THIEVES I'VE KNOWN

EST. 75 YEARS 1938

THE UNIVERSITY OF GEORGIA PRESS 2013

FLANNERY
O'CONNOR
AWARD
FOR
SHORT
FICTION

Nancy Zafris,
Series Editor

THIEVES

I'VE

KNOWN

STORIES

TOM

KEALEY

THE UNIVERSITY

OF GEORGIA PRESS

ATHENS AND

LONDON

Published by the University of Georgia Press
Athens, Georgia 30602
www.ugapress.org
© 2013 by Tom Kealey
All rights reserved
Designed by Kaelin Chappell Broaddus
Set in 9.5/14 Quadraat Regular
by Graphic Composition, Inc.,
Bogart, Georgia
Printed and bound by Sheridan Books, Inc.
The paper in this book meets the guidelines
for permanence and durability of the
Committee on Production Guidelines for
Book Longevity of the
Council on Library Resources.

Printed in the United States of America
17 16 15 14 13 C 5 4 3 2 1

Library of Congress
Cataloging-in-Publication Data
Kealey, Tom.
Thieves I've known : stories / by Tom Kealey.
pages cm. — (Winner of the Flannery
O'Connor Award for Short Fiction)
ISBN-13: 978-0-8203-4537-6
(hardcover : alk. paper)
ISBN-10: 0-8203-4537-7
(hardcover : alk. paper)
I. Title.
PS3611.E146 2013
813'.6—dc23
2012049542

British Library Cataloging-in-Publication
Data available

To Helen, Jack, and Kerri

And to the Kealey

and Carroll families

CONTENTS

THIEVES
I'VE
KNOWN

Many of my favorite

things are broken.

MARIO BUATTA

INTRODUCTION, OR NOBODY

Nights at the store, the brother and sister bagged the groceries that tumbled down the conveyors, rarely looking up, a simple nod of the head at a thanks from a customer. The girl, Merrill, was fifteen and tall for her age. The brother, Nate, was sixteen and trying to grow a moustache. He often wore a green knit hat. They didn't talk much with the cashiers or the manager. A yes sir, no ma'am here and there. When the store was slow, they brought in the carts, held contests between each other: who could bring in the most. Other times, one of them would take the broom and move down the aisles, collecting the candy wrappers, the spilled sugar, the vegetable leaves in the produce corner, while the other rotated stock, made the shelves look full. They had a rubber ball, the size of a tennis ball but bright red, that they played a game with, sometimes down an empty aisle and sometimes in the parking lot. There were rules involved in the game, it was clear to the manager the times he watched them: the number of bounces, the left or right hand that they sometimes grabbed with, sometimes slapped back. Often enough, they simply rolled the ball to each other, set it to strange spins, and after, they would hold up fingers—between two and five, he could never predict. When he asked the girl about the rules, she simply blushed and looked at the floor, like she'd been caught stealing something.

It was late summer, almost autumn, and after work they'd play other games in the parking lot, and the manager would watch them out there while counting his receipts, marking up the inventory for the next day. They'd ride a shopping cart down the hill, one inside the cage, other times the both of them hanging off the back. For all their games, they rarely smiled, and something about the way they held themselves reminded the manager of his brother, who had died as a child. He'd been younger by many years than these two. They would often bounce the red ball over top the manager's car—one of the few left in the lot at that hour—and he considered each time to go out and chase them off. But he was afraid they might take it harder than he'd intended, like his younger brother had taken things, and other than the games they gave him no trouble, which was rare for his workers.

Merrill and Nate were not aware that they were watched. The windows at the office were dark, and they could see only the dull lit aisles in the store, the stillness inside. Often, they'd watch the heat lightning in the sky, the red blip of the radio tower beyond the tree line, a small and slow airplane headed miles toward the country runway. This night, a small bat skipped around the glow of the streetlamps, searching for the night bugs that were also drawn there. Nate found the smallest of pebbles and began tossing them up at the lights, and the bat would swoop and dive at what the boy threw, catching the small stone for a moment, then dropping it again. Merrill watched them both.

"You try it," Nate said to her.

"Why?"

"Because a rock is like a big bug to him."

"But not when he catches it."

This response annoyed him. "So?" he said.

"So, would you tease a blind person?"

He frowned. "Don't be a dolt."

"You're the dolt."

"Oh, that's clever," he said.

He tossed a few more, and eventually the bat figured out the game. They collected the rest of the carts, though their shift was over, set them in a line near the front door. After, they could hear the deep whistle of a train from beyond the back of the store, through the narrow woods, the bells of the crossing signals, the rumble of boxcars along the tracks. They picked up their aprons and box cutters from the sidewalk and headed that way. It put Nate in mind of a story he'd once heard: a deaf girl picking flowers too close to the tracks. He named her Klara in his mind, as he and his sister picked their way through the line of trees toward the train. His mother had told him that story as a warning, though she'd left out the name. He thought about the engineer in the locomotive, and what he must've been thinking, looking down the tracks at the girl. The man must have pulled and pulled at the horn, and the boy tried to figure if the man understood her as deaf after a time, or just without sense. Hadn't the girl felt the vibrations of the tracks? There was no answer, but the boy liked to think about these things: at what point the man had punched the brakes. The boy thought of the man, thinking. The number of cars behind him and the distance ahead to the girl.

They waited, watched the dark boxcars and the rounded petroleum tankers pass, felt the rumble beneath their feet and the breeze, which smelled of coal and grease, at their faces. As the last car passed, they watched the cloud of dust and grit that settled behind it, the moon ahead, low. It seemed that the train might be headed there.

Across the tracks and into the next line of trees. They found the creek that they could jump and the ditch that they couldn't. Their feet slipped in the dirt and mud, and they picked mosquitoes and thorns from their necks and arms.

The cemetery was beyond the woods, and in the starlight it often looked like a miniature city to them: buildings and roads, shadows that somebody could hide in. They hopped the gate, watched the sculptures as they passed: an angel here, like a child, an eagle and an owl sitting together there. The first time, they'd thought the owl real. They stopped at the largest angel, the one not like a child, just before the lane of unmarked graves. The angel was tall and dark and skeletal, and it held a large sword above its head. In the moonlight they could see the jagged teeth and the empty eye sockets. The mouth looked like it was ready to scream bloody murder, or commit it, and they didn't consider it much like anything they'd like to meet in heaven. They stood watching it for a while, as they always did, nudging each other with a finger or an elbow, trying to work up a scare.

Merrill tried to make a scary voice. She moaned. "Bring me back my eyes."

Nate set his hands in his pockets. He watched the clouds behind the statue, kept an eye on the length of the sword, the broken tip at the end.

"Did you see it move?" said Merrill. Her voice seemed to indicate that it was important that he did.

"If it'll make you happy I'll say that I did," he said.

But honestly, it always seemed to move a little, so they walked on, poked each other some more as they made their way past the gravestones. Merrill stopped and straightened a cluster of dead flowers that had been knocked over. When they came to the unmarked graves, they both thought of the ghost stories: one of the cashiers had told them this. When the ghosts were alive, generations ago, they'd worked in a textile mill, south of the town, and then they were burned up in a fire. The mill was made of bricks, and there were no windows, and the foreman—examining the remains—couldn't tell one worker from the other. Immigrants, they were believed to be, and no one came to claim the bodies. So, they got buried here, in a long line, with just the date of their deaths. If you walked close enough, they'd reach up and grab you, and they'd steal your name. This is how the story went. And after that, you were just nobody. Nate kept his distance, but Merrill walked close enough, felt that they could have her name if it would do them some good. But neither ever walked right over them.

They hopped the far gate after that and headed east.

They were miles from the Sound and from home, but they were getting closer. The smell of salt water was in the air. At a familiar neighborhood, Merrill and Nate balanced on the curb as they walked, made their way around garbage cans and mailboxes, took three steps each in the driveways. A few dogs barked from backyards, and they could see their shadows at the fence lines. They passed all sorts of things in yards: cars with hoods up, no engines inside; lawn chairs here and there; a mower in a yard with no grass; and once a pyramid of beer bottles set on wooden boards. In one driveway they passed a pair of boots, empty, but pointed out at the road, like they were waiting for the owner to return.

They listened to the static of radios here and there, somebody running an electric saw in a garage. It put Merrill in mind of their previous home, years ago, when they'd lived with their mother, where Merrill and Nate would often enough sit at the kitchen table alone, listening to the rattle of the old refrigerator.

Lights were on in houses, though often curtains were drawn, and from the curb Merrill and Nate began to imagine what might be happening inside each house. This was a game they often played. It was almost all guesses. They couldn't see much.

"Somebody's in love," said Nate, pointing at the first chosen house.

"Somebody's coming out of it," said Merrill toward the second.

"Some woman playing checkers by herself."

"A pair of men, watching baseball, naked."

"That's good," said Nate. "I like that one." He waited for the next house, tried to think up something to top it. "Somebody hiding a body."

"A human body?"

"Yes, a human body."

"You've done that one before."

"All right," he said. "Somebody chopping one up, then. Feet first."

"Blech," said Merrill. They rounded a corner and went up another street. She waited as they walked. It was important not to get too far ahead.

"Some child escaping a bath," she said. "But he's not going to be able to escape it forever."

Nate looked at the next house. It was small, and there were no lights on. The windows were all shut, but the front door was open.

"There's some parent waiting up there," he said. "Trying to keep their kid alive."

They listened to the dogs as Merrill considered. Above them, the moths and the night bugs hovered around the streetlamps. The next house was all lit up, and they could see people inside, about a half dozen, more in other rooms.

"They're all waiting for some woman to make them a sandwich," said Merrill.

They watched the people as they passed the house. It seemed as if there might be some somber occasion happening inside.

"What kind of sandwich?"

"Different kinds," she said. "There's not enough turkey to go around, so she's using some leftover breakfast sausage. She's cutting it up into thin slices. There's also an avocado, and there's a visitor to the house who's never had an avocado. He likes it. He tries to grow avocados when he gets back home, but he's not successful. He takes it as a defect in his character."

"He sounds like a loser," says Nate.

Merrill shrugs. "I like him," she says.

"Why is it the woman making the sandwiches?" says Nate. "Why can't the men make their own sandwiches?"

Merrill almost crosses her arms. But she keeps them at her sides. She rolls her eyes. "We're three houses behind."

Nate stops. He closes his eyes. He stands military straight. He's got bad posture and is overaccounting for it. He looks like someone about to do a backflip. "In the first house there are three people watching television. It's a show about making little chairs. Little-kid chairs. The daughter, a teenager, thinks, that's what I'd like to do when I grow up, make little-kid chairs. The other two people don't take her very seriously. But she's serious. She meets a carpenter. She meets a lot of carpenters. They teach her what they know. She's not very good at first, but she gets better as she goes along. She starts making these little-kid chairs. She puts an ad in the newspaper. She'll make your kid a little chair, and she'll even paint the kid's name on the chair. But when parents arrive, there's something about the chairs that they don't like. There's something, to their surprise, a little creepy about the chairs. Something says to them, some voice, it says, don't put your kid's name on any of these chairs. The voice seems to indicate that something really bad will happen if they do."

Merrill breathes in deep. "You are so weird," she says.

"I'm not done," Nate says. His eyes are still closed. "So she's stuck with all these creepy little chairs in her house. Even she thinks they're creepy. Her boyfriend, he has a hairy back, and one day he'll be her husband. He likes the chairs, and he likes her. But she wants to be done with those chairs. She takes them out to the curb one day to get rid of them all."

Merrill interjects. "But even the garbage men don't like the chairs."

"Absolutely," says Nate. "Those garbage men are scared too. They want to leave the chairs there. But they pick them up and crush them in the compactor. They smash them until those chairs can't hurt anybody anymore."

"That's a great story," says Merrill.

"I'm not done yet," says Nate.

"We're going to be here all night."

"I know for a fact you have nothing better to do."

"Don't be so sure, but go on."

Nate opens his eyes. "So, she gives up chair-making. She makes hats. It's a lot less work and less creepy too. She eventually starts her own business, through mail order. It's called Tippy's Hats. Though that's not her name. Tippy. It's just what she calls the business. It's a hit."

Merrill waits. She watches him.

Nate shrugs. "That's all," he says.

She sometimes thinks her brother is crazy, and this greatly endears him to her. She knows that she's crazy. He's her only true friend in the world.

"There's a man who owns four birds in the next house," she says. "All day long he talks to his birds, hoping they'll talk back to him. But they're not talking birds. They're finches and canaries. They never say a word. He lives a life of great disappointment."

Nate nods at the next house. "The woman there is in love with the bird man. She thinks it's great, how he talks to his birds. But he hardly notices her, even though she brings him tomatoes. Most weeks of every summer, she brings him a half-dozen tomatoes. To him, though, she's just the tomato lady."

They walk on.

"This is suddenly depressing," says Merrill.

"It's your turn," says Nate. "Lift us up."

She thinks about that. She hops over the lid of a garbage can.

"The husband of an astronaut lives there," she says. "His wife is in outer space, but there's a problem with the spaceship. We're all worried about her. The Earth is. We're all worried about her and five others in the spaceship. There's some door in the spaceship that won't close, and they can't come back to Earth if that door won't close. No one wants to say it, but they're going to run out of oxygen.

"The husband," Merrill continues, "he has a lover. It's a man. It's a man he knew when they were both in high school, and in the last year they've reconnected. The husband is surprised about all this, but when he's with his lover he's not surprised at all. On the fourth day of the crisis in space, he understands a clear truth: his wife is going to die by the end of the week. She's dying right now as he's thinking this. He's overcome with guilt. He loves her very much. And, at the same time, and he's not proud of this, he's happy. Because now he can be who he is. In fact, he already is who he is."

Merrill looks over at her brother. He has stepped off the curb and is walking beside her now. She can tell by the way that he moves that this is the last story of the night.

"Go ahead," Nate says. "I want to hear the finish."

Merrill keeps walking but steps down off the curb too. "The next evening, the door closes. The door in outer space closes. One of the astronauts had a good idea. All five of them now, they're going to make it back just fine. The husband, he lies in bed with his lover. The two people that he loves most in the world are alive. This makes him feel alive. He feels like his heart is going to jump out of his chest and burn the house to the ground. Bad times are ahead, but he's happy for the first time in his life. When his lover starts to snore, it doesn't bother the husband as much as it used to. He doesn't notice the noise so much. He notices his lover's breath moving in and out."

Nate kicks a soda can. He puts his hands back in his pockets. Merrill has worked on that story all week. She has tried to get it just right. Having told it now, she feels like the second half started to fall apart. She should've left out the snoring part. She looks at her watch. It's almost midnight.

Nate looks ahead. There are a few more houses, though their father's trailer is still a mile past this neighborhood. Nate spits. This is a habit he has taken up recently. It annoys Merrill to no end. She suddenly shivers. It's cold out. The stories—especially the creepy chair story for some reason—had kept her warm. She feels as if a thin ghost has passed very quickly and uncomfortably through her. When she remembers this walk, years later, she'll remember Nate as the one with the shivers.

"Do you think they're watching us?" she says.

"Who?"

She points up at the houses. "The people in there."

Nate shrugs. "Why would they bother?"

"It might be interesting for them." Merrill considers the light in the windows. "We seem as if we're just outside, but we're actually far, far away."

FROM BREMERTON

Shelby woke before sunrise, dressed in her warmest clothes in the dark. In the kitchen, she packed her book bag with apples and bread, some peanut butter. She added a map of Seattle, a carton of cigarettes she'd hidden at the top of a cabinet, and then brewed some coffee on the stove. She walked barefoot in the trailer so as not to wake her sister and the boyfriend. It was still dark outside by the time she poured the coffee into her thermos, and out through the window she could see the dull yellow glow of a streetlamp at the edge of the trailer park. Rain fell in the lamp glow, and she could hear the drops clicking against the top of the trailer. She wished she were back in bed, but she'd made a promise the week before, to a boy that she was in love with, although she was not now sure if she was still in love. Lots of things—her love for the boy, her grades in school, her future, or what she hoped to be her future—were in doubt. Wisps of fog disappeared in the rain. Before leaving, and because it was her nature, she put away the beer cans and the pizza boxes from the night before, emptied the ashtrays, wiped down the counters. She slipped into her boots, pulled her woolen cap over her ears, and closed the door, quietly, on her way out.

In the puddles of mud and slush outside she caught a blurred, distant reflection of her own gaze, a reflection that she liked: dark and small, without many features, a work in progress it seemed. She stepped around the puddles when she could, leaning over them, kicking a soda bottle across the park, listening to the rattle across rocks and broken glass. Outside Phillip's trailer, she could see a light on in the kitchen. A cat, wet and muddy, eyed her from under a small porch as she made her way toward the light.

She knocked, listened to a series of loud thumps from inside the trailer, entered when no one came to the door. Inside, Phillip knelt in a corner holding a shoe above his head. A dozen or so brown splotches—roaches—were scattered on the floor around him. The kitchen smelled of mold and baked chicken.

Phillip turned as she slid a chair out from the table and sat down. His eyes were large, a little irregular, and his bony elbows and wrists seemed like knots on a straight line. He was not a good-looking boy, but Shelby—who was similarly thin, and who'd had painful acne since she was twelve—could find the beautiful parts of him when she put her mind to it. His hair, which was long and smelled of smoke and lemon soap, his lips, his neck and fingers. She liked all of these things, and liked him. Believed him to be good, if not good-looking. She felt a turn in her breathing as she sat watching his large eyes. The boy reached into his pocket, took out a roll of dollar bills, tossed them to her.

"How much?" she said.

"Enough to get us there."

Under the streetlamp, they sat on an overturned apple crate, watched the first blue-pink rays of the sun appear from across the water. The Olympic Mountains were snow-capped and gray. A half-dozen men and one woman sat on similar crates, on seats torn from old cars. One old man drank from a coffee mug, the steam fogging the man's glasses each time he sipped. Nothing was said. They all watched the road that led from the trailer park, and those that had them shielded themselves from the rain with umbrellas. Others wore ponchos. Phillip and Shelby sat under a plastic trash bag cut lengthwise down the sides. Phillip slipped a square sheet of white paper from his pocket, unfolded it on his knee. He creased new lines as he refolded it in triangles from each corner, bent those folds inside out and down until he'd made what looked like a fisherman's rain cap. The man with the coffee mug watched him. Phillip folded two opposite corners together, and then the remaining corners up, folded what was left in half, pressed his finger against the angles to keep the creases. He set the paper right side up and placed it on Shelby's knee.

"What's that?" said the old man.

"It's a sailboat," said Shelby.

The man squinted and looked doubtful. The woman next to him stamped her boots in the mud, for warmth it seemed, still looking down the road. Behind her, in the distance, the pine trees swayed with the wind.

Shelby placed the sailboat at the edge of one of the puddles, flicked it lightly with her finger. The paper turned back at the motion, the bow pointing up at the sky, but the vessel floated in the red water.

"Nice trick," said the man. He pulled his poncho closer around his shoulders. "Maybe you can make a roof next."

Shelby picked up the sailboat, shook out the water as best she could. She unfolded the sail first, watched Phillip out of the corner of her eye as he shook his head. He'd taught her the next folds the week before. She liked that about him: he knew things, even if it was only paper folding and the like. He'd made a compass from a needle and magnet, Halloween masks from feathers, glue, and cardboard. He knew how to draw well and seemed content to teach her what she could learn. She doubled the paper back, refolded the sail, and turned the bow of the boat inside itself. She took out a pen. In the center of the fold she drew a dot within a circle, added some waved lines and shading at the bird's neck.

She looked over at the man.

"A dinosaur?" he said.

"A rooster."

"Hmm."

In the distance, the headlights of a pickup truck appeared through the fog. The woman stood up from the crate and shook out her umbrella, but the men stayed seated, looked out through the rain. Phillip unfolded the rooster, set the paper flat on his knee again, tore slits along some of the folds. They listened to a dog bark in the distance.

When the truck entered the park, they could see three men already in the back huddled against the wooden slats and a driver, sitting alone, in the cab. Rainwater kicked from the tires. Phillip folded and refolded as the truck approached the collection of crates and the window rolled down. A bearded man peered out into the rain.

"I got work for four. Bring you back around eight."

"How much?" said the woman.

"Fifty."

"What're we to do?" she said.

He pointed his thumb at her. "Not you then. I'll take three of you men and the boy. Decide and get in."

The woman sat back down on the crate, gave the man a look, although there'd likely be other trucks to come along. The old man and two others shook out their ponchos and umbrellas and climbed into the back of the truck. One of the men remaining lit a cigarette.

"You give my friend a lift?" said Phillip. "Wherever we're going?"

"Going where I always take you," the man said. "I said I'd pay for four, now get in or get out."

"No pay," said Phillip. "Just a lift."

The man shifted the truck into gear. "If there's room," he said. The window rolled up.

In the back of the truck, Shelby and Phillip stood against the cab, tried to hold the plastic bag against the wind as the truck made its way up the road. The backs of their shirts were wet through their jackets, and they shivered with the cold. In the gray wood, previous workers had carved their initials or nicknames. A few hearts were scattered here and there between the cracks, an etching of an airplane. Next to Shelby's head, an inscription read *Tony hates Eloise.*

"Hey," Phillip said to the man with the coffee mug. "You got any kids?"

The man looked up out of his poncho. "What's that to you?"

Phillip took out the piece of folded paper, handed it down. The man took it with the tips of his fingers, turned it over in his hands, examined it.

"Brontosaurus," he said.

"Sure."

"They're likely to swallow it," the man said, but he slipped the paper into his shirt pocket.

During the ride, Shelby imagined a truck much like this, one in her future perhaps, a warmer ride even in Alaska. It would be summertime, and she'd be headed west from the train station in Anchorage, to work the fish lines in a small harbor town. She'd picked some of these towns out on a map, names that she liked: Kasilof, Ninilchik, Port Graham; and she'd read a slim book by a woman who'd done what Shelby hoped to do: worked the lines in the summers, saved her money in the winters, invested in a boat after that—the woman, like Shelby, was no fisher-woman, she'd had others work for her—made her fortune and was mak-ing more. The woman, like Shelby, liked the water. Phillip thought it a strange, unlikely wish.

"This woman made it," Shelby'd said.

"Make sure you read about the ones that didn't," he'd said.

They rode the seven miles toward Bremerton, caught a glimpse of the bay during one stretch, the vessels making their way down Saratoga Pass. The rain fell harder the closer they came. Eventually the men made some room and the two teenagers knelt against the cab, covered their heads with the plastic, watched the raindrops through the thin black covering. The light of the sky was becoming a brighter gray.

In Bremerton, they jumped out at a traffic stop, waved back at the men in the truck, who stared dully after them. They cut down an alley-way, past a diner window fogged up from the rain, past the lines of ships moored at the docks, their white masts bobbing in the air like a row of birthday candles, past the stacks of netting. In the ferry terminal they opened a pack from the cigarette carton, lit up, counted out their money. Phillip paid at the counter for his ticket, boarded alone. Shelby waited on the dock, out of sight, she hoped, behind a wall of crab traps and crates. On the ferry, Phillip rolled his ticket stub into a ball, leaned over the rail-ing, looked behind him. He'd hoped to be sly, but he looked guilty as the damned. He threw the stub out over the water, just a few yards, wondered if he'd been spotted. Shelby found the balled stub in a crack between the crates, slipped her hand inside, nabbed it between the tips of her two longest fingers. She held her breath at the gate, held up the ticket, folded flat but looking worn and wet. The teenager, about Shelby's age, looked to get out of the rain, waved her on, tore the next ticket.

They sat in the cabin, sharing coffee from the thermos, set their socks and sweaters across a bench to dry. They watched the flag at the stern flap in the wind as the ferry pulled out from the bay, headed into the pass, watched the gulls and terns gliding behind the fishing boats headed in the same direction. She'd brought paper, Shelby, and they practiced the folds to pass the time. Made the fish, the baby starling, the teacup, and the seven-pointed star. A young girl sat across from them, next to her mother. Though Halloween had passed, the girl wore a grinning skeleton mask. Her eyes looked wide through the holes, and as Shelby and Phillip completed each figure, each animal or structure, she slipped the mask to the top of her head, hugged the toy elephant doll she held in her hands, looked away and then back again at the folded paper set next to the socks and sweaters. Then the girl pulled the mask back down over her face.

"You're scary looking," said Phillip.

"So are you," said the girl.

The girl's mother flipped through a magazine, not taking her eyes from the pages. At one point she handed the girl a peppermint and a napkin. The other passengers, few this time of year, looked out on the water or walked out to the deck, feet spread wide with the dip and roll of the vessel. A radio hummed with static, not music but news, a buzz of quiet voices discussing stocks and markets, bills and pending deals. White spray from the water splashed against the decks and the windows.

"Would you like one of these?" said Shelby. She pointed at the folded papers.

"Depends which one," said the girl.

"You can pick it."

The girl pushed her mask up to her forehead again. She looked up at her mother for a moment and then back at the line of figures. She

ignored the fish and the boot, the cube and the starling. She eyed the
teacup.

"I'll take the star," she said.

"Go get it," said Shelby.

The girl slid off the bench, pressed her feet against the floor, hesitated, and then took two steps to the opposite bench. She held her elephant doll tight, then touched one of the sweaters for a moment, and
then took her hand away. She clicked her tongue while deciding and
took both the star and the teacup, then returned to her own side, leaning
against her mother.

"I like your elephant," said Shelby.

"You can't have it."

"I didn't say I wanted it. I just like it."

The girl turned the elephant's face toward her, examined it. "I left the
good one at home," she said.

In the Seattle terminal, they waited, wanting to stay warm. Outside, the
rain had not let up, gave no sign that it would. They ate an apple each,
shared a sandwich, wiped the peanut butter from each other's lips.
Shelby hoped she might find answers to questions on the boy's lips, with
her finger, wondered if he might be thinking the same thing. They said
little though, were comfortable and intrigued with each other's silence.
Phillip brought out a long plastic garbage bag and they tore it in half, a
side sheltering each, and walked out into the rain.

They looked for street signs and examined Shelby's map in the doorway of a bookstore, walked along the dock, staring out at the large black-
and-red tankers, the smaller fishing boats, the yachts in the harbor in the
rain. A rope trailed after a ship, tied to the stern like a long, thick water
snake. Phillip thought about Shelby's eyes, which he liked. He thought
about a lot of things: his mother, who they were going to see, his roll
of money in his pocket, the skeleton mask on the girl on the ferryboat.
In his notebook he'd drawn similar masks, but they were the faces of
aliens, not skeletons, although he saw the resemblance now. When he
could afford it, he rented old movies—anything science fiction—read

dime novels from the used book store on 7th Street. He watched the sky at night. What would they be like? He drew robots and three-headed creatures, hovering cubes and giant eyes. Then, reading more, he'd become serious. If they came, they'd be near to humans—would appear in that form at least. He was not completely certain, but had settled on this theory, not his own, but read in books.

He thought about the aliens a lot. Thought they might seek him out—not just him, but all the people who believed. He sketched and sketched in his notebook. His mother, when she'd lived with him, thought the drawings foolish. The faces were smooth and expressionless, the limbs he didn't know about—how many and how long—but the eyes, dark and deep, were warm in his drawings. Eyes looking for an answer, scientific but not unfeeling. He thought he might wait another year, believing. After that, he'd have to give it up. He believed, but he didn't have faith. It was a problem, he felt, that he had in many areas. Sometimes, he thought life might not be out there after all, and if it was, it might not visit him.

They found the address in a phone booth, shared a cigarette inside the glass, kept out of the rain. After, they found the barbershop on James Street, a shop away from the corner, but they could only make out shapes—people sitting, the motion of hands—through the fogged window.

Inside, they sat down in a row of chairs under a television, kept their eyes on the floor at first, watching the strands of hair turn in the puddles of water, listening to the buzz of a razor, the click of scissors.

"Be with you in a minute," said the barber.

The man's head was bald, but he had a full gray beard, thick and clipped at the sideburns and moustache, thin on the chin. He chewed on a toothpick. One of his eyes was gray also, looked damaged in the glow of the fluorescent lights. The customer had his eyes closed, seemed asleep as the barber held the hair between index and middle fingers, snipped some away. A newspaper lay open on the seat next to Shelby, but she watched the reflection of the television in the mirror behind the barber. As they waited the president walked down a ramp from a helicopter, and a crowd, at night, stood outside a building billowing smoke. Two women swam through floodwater in a red river, and an astronaut floated in zero gravity. Space was dark and open behind him. On Earth, a young boy in an orange jumpsuit was led away in shackles, hand and foot.

They listened to the slap of customers' shoes in the puddle near the door, waited for the bell to ring in the frame. The barber toweled off his hands, set his money in a drawer.

"Which one or both?" he said.

"You know Carney Booth?" said Shelby.

The man set the towel on the chair, closed the lid over the damaged eye for a moment, looked Shelby up and down, then Phillip.

"I might," he said. "Who's asking?"

"A friend."

"There's a few types of friends out in the world. Which kind would you be?"

"My sister's his girlfriend."

The barber nodded. "Seems like he might have a few of those."

"Maybe," said Shelby. "But I got one of his favors to call in."

"What kind of favor'd you give him?"

Shelby looked over at Phillip, who kept his gaze at the floor.

"Your name's Otis," she said to the man.

"You could read that on the window outside."

"You were army buddies."

"Navy."

"Then you know him?"

"I knew a man named Carney," the man said. "I'm not sure about a favor, though. What are you asking for?"

"A lift up to Rawlins. Just take an hour, far as I can tell."

The man considered. "Two hours there, two hours back. Take up most of my day."

"We've got to be there at three, but we'll get back on our own."

The man turned his head, as if he was refiguring the conversation. "Nothing but a prison up there," he said.

"That's right."

"You visiting?"

"That's right."

"Who?" said the man.

Shelby nudged Phillip. "My mom," the boy said.

"What's she in for?"

Phillip said nothing, shrugged.

"Am I mumbling?" said the man.

"No sir," said Phillip. "Drugs."

The man picked up the towel from the chair and sat down, set his feet up on the stand.

"What's so interesting about that floor?" he said.

Shelby glanced at Phillip but said nothing.

"Something more interesting than the person you're talking to?"

They looked up at him, turned their eyes away for a moment, then looked again.

"You don't like my eye," he said.

"It's fine," said Shelby.

"It scares you."

"No sir."

"I'm old enough to know a lie when I hear it," he said.

They looked at his eye. A gray film seemed to cover it, and beyond the film, the pupil took away the color, seemed to bleed into the white. It was neither menacing nor warm, only there, staring at them. Phillip wondered what the man could see.

"It scares me a little," he said.

The man looked out the window, at the bell at the top of the door frame. They listened for the sound, Shelby and Phillip, aimed their own eyes back to the floor, watched the hair float in the puddle.

"You'll get used to it," the man said. "I have."

They drove out the highway north, took a two-lane road from there, past the lumber mills with the saws and the stacks of cottonwood trees and the lines of trucks idling at the loading docks. Shelby sat in the back-seat of the car, listened to the strum of an acoustic guitar from the tape player. Through the window, through the rain, she saw the lights of a high school, could see the heads of students in a classroom, computers against the wall, a large gymnasium next to the school. She could not make out faces, but the students seemed like they were going places, the way they held themselves. She felt far away from Bremerton, missed it, like you'd miss the humidity of summer, the bone cold of rain in a truck headed toward the coastline, missed the voices of people you liked but didn't quite trust.

She could see the eyes of the man in the rearview mirror.

"You like this music?" he said.

Shelby listened. It sounded rough, static in the background. The guitar player seemed as if he didn't know where he was headed with the riff, with the melody, seemed as if he'd stay awhile where he was.

"This is your playing."

The man set his eyes back on the road. "That's right. You didn't an-swer the question, though."

"I like it."

"I told you I know a lie when I hear one."

"You're not knowing one now," she said.

"I'm not sure," he said. "I'm deciding."

Phillip warmed his hands at the vents, turned his hands over and under at the hot air. He felt inside his jacket for the present he'd wrapped for his mother, felt the square of the package, the corners and the crinkle of paper.

The man shifted the toothpick in his mouth. "What's Carney up to?" he said.

"Works at the courthouse," said Shelby.

"Where?"

"Bremerton."

"Good lord," said the man. "What's he do there?"

"Janitor."

The man nodded. "That sounds right. You tell him hello for me?"

"I'll tell him."

"I could tell you some stories," said Otis.

"Is that right?"

"Yep," he said.

Shelby waited. They passed mile markers on the right, a rail bridge where a line of tankers and boxcars sat overhead, a reservoir that stretched for as far as Shelby could see. The man said nothing, told no stories.

"Can I ask you something?" Shelby said.

"All right."

"What kind of favor you owe him for?"

The man shrugged. "He got me some dope or something. Not even sure it was him. I got a vague recollection he's got something coming, but I can't name it. Let that be a lesson to both of you. Write down your favors so you'll remember."

They drove on, listening to the whirr of the wipers, the tap of rain on the windshield, the guitar on the tape deck as it cut off, flipped, played the other side. The man's guitar skill was not good, Shelby thought, but not bad either. He seemed to know when to pause, knew the space between chords, knew the right notes if not the combinations. Phillip took out a sheet of paper from his back pocket, set it flat against his knee, set it like he'd set the others, began to tear and fold.

"Borrow your toothpick?" he said to the man.

"My toothpick?"

"That's right."

The man drove on for a while, looked at Shelby in the rearview mirror, closed the lid over the damaged eye. He slipped out the pick, handed it to the boy.

Phillip folded, ripped away some paper, took out a penknife and cut slits in the folds, stuck in the toothpick. They drove on. When he was done, Phillip set the paper guitar on the dashboard, lengthwise, pointing the neck toward the man, the toothpick sitting in for the strings.

"How much longer you got in school?" said the man.

"A year for me," said Shelby. "After this one. Two for him."

"Where you headed after that?"

"Who says we're headed anywhere?"

"Everybody, as far as I hear, heads out of Bremerton."

"You been?"

"Out?" said the man. "Or Bremerton?"

"Both then."

Otis picked up the guitar from the dashboard, set it on top of the steering wheel.

"In the navy, Carney and I saw Germany and Japan, Hawaii and the tip of Greenland. We got off the ship when we could. You wonder, what you see in a port town, and what that tells of the rest of the place. I've seen thirteen countries and four continents, but I'd like to see more. Bremerton I've seen, took the ferry out. My wife and I like the water. I've seen worse and I've seen better. Have I been out? That's a good question. I've been out, but I'm not sure if I've been in."

The man turned the wheel, and the guitar slid off onto the floor. On a straightaway, he leaned forward and felt at the floorboard, found the paper and set it back on the dash. He wiped his fist at the window to clear off the mist.

"That's a fine guitar," he said.

As the rain tapered to a drizzle, the breeze from the coastline picked up, bending trees over power lines, blowing sand and black wet leaves across the road. When it was offered, Otis took an apple from the book bag and after set the core next to the guitar on the dashboard. The dull glow of the sun—still behind clouds—began its descent toward the Olympics, and shadows stretched out from barns and shacks, from the clusters of sheep and goats behind fences. Phillip creased and folded more paper, making a shark, then a lighthouse, though not a good one. He unfolded, started over, made a frog that he set on Shelby's hand.

"We got a trick on this one," she said.

"What's that?" said Otis.

Shelby pushed down on the back tip of the frog, pressed it to the edge of the seat top, let her finger go. The frog hopped forward, landing head-first between the boy and the man.

Otis looked down and studied the frog. "Y'all don't have much to do out in Bremerton, do you?" he said.

"It's for luck," said Phillip. "Frogs bring it."

"That right?"

"You got a frog in your garden, it means something good's going on."

"How about in your car?"

"Same I suppose."

The man picked up the frog and set it next to the guitar, next to the apple core.

"We're about there," the man said. "How long's this visit?"

"A couple hours," said Phillip. "We're catching a bus back. You did your favor and then some."

Ahead, they could see a stoplight and what served as a town—a market and a post office, a boarded-up restaurant named Billy's. A man passed them on the sidewalk, kept his raincoat closed against the wind. Otis slowed the car and stopped at the light.

"It isn't my business to ask, but how long's your mom in for?"

"Five years," said Phillip.

"And how much of that she done?"

"One, a little more."

"She sold?"

"We lived in a house that sold. Same thing before the judge."

"She could've pled that down," said Otis. "I know that business."

Phillip looked out at the market on the corner. "She wouldn't testify against her boyfriend, so they sent her down."

"Love?" said Otis.

Phillip considered that. "Didn't seem like it."

The man shifted into first when the light changed. "Maybe not to you," he said. "Bet they were keen on sending you to a home."

"I been to a home last year in Tacoma."

Otis looked over at Phillip. "Not even a deal for you?"

"Not from them."

"But your mom could've pulled one."

Phillip stared out the window. Up ahead, Shelby could see the towers of the prison, the wire and the fences, a concrete square, ugly and dark like the sky. She closed up her book bag and zipped her jacket.

"I think I've answered more than I had to," said Phillip.

"All right," said Otis. "I got somewhere I didn't mean to go."

The man circled the prison block, looked out through the drizzle and the gray light. He found the parking lot and the entranceway to the gate. A line of people—visitors, old men and women, lots of young children—stood under an aluminum rooftop, dressed for cold and wet. A guard in a green slicker stood behind the fence.

Phillip slipped his fingers into the door latch but didn't open. Shelby waited on him.

"Y'all can stay dry here till it's time to go."

"We've kept you long enough," said Phillip. "Thanks for the ride."

They got out, stood in the drizzle as they collected their things. The air was cold and heavy, and the wind blew sand in their eyes and hair.

Otis leaned forward, pointed at the dashboard. "You forgot your little doo-dad."

"That's for you," said Phillip. "That frog'll make something good happen."

"I'll believe that when I see it," said the man.

They closed their doors and watched as the car moved past the line of people, heading toward the exit near the state road. One of the brake lights flickered like a dim red sparkler, and the windows were fogged over in the side and back. They couldn't see Otis anymore, not the eye or the gray. They stood in the drizzle with their packs, brushed the sand from their own eyes, then walked to the rooftop, waited at the back of the line.

In the greeting room, families fanned out to the line of benches, rows against the cinder-block walls and down the center. Outside, they'd

stood quiet in the drizzle, listening to the raindrops ping against the
aluminum rooftop. But inside there was a faint buzz of voices, eyes set
on the clock on the wall. Grime and dust caked the windows. The room
smelled of disinfectant and coffee. Children played with toy trucks and
cars, blocks and electronic games, some on the floor, others on top of
benches. A pall of smoke drifted up toward the ceiling as grandparents
and a few fathers lit up cigarettes, listened for the turn of the lock at the
far door, told their kids to quiet down.

Phillip took out the boxed present from his jacket, set it at the edge of
their bench. Shelby was unsure of what to do. She thought about the bus
station she'd seen on one of her maps, but hadn't spotted it on the way
into town. She tried to keep her mind on the present, took hold of Phillip's hand and rubbed at his middle knuckle. He kept still, kept his hand
in hers. Above them, the rows of lights buzzed and hummed, echoed
against the high ceiling. Phillip looked lost.

"I thought you'd been before," she said.

"I never said that."

She looked down at his hand. "You want to draw something?"

"No."

"I got a notebook in the bag."

"You can take that carton out if you want."

She unzipped the bag, reached past the bread and the maps, took out
the cigarettes. As the lock turned, the sound echoed above the pitch of
the lights. The children stopped their play at the trucks and blocks, at the
games. Men stubbed out their cigarettes. A tall guard came out the door,
followed by the first of the prisoners.

Phillip and Shelby watched them come. They were each dressed in
red, the women, all of them with their hair tied back or shaved short.
Some were old, gray, others little older than Shelby. They walked in
single file, then spread, some running, some walking to the tables. An
older prisoner put her glasses on. There were hugs, a shriek of delight
here or there. A few simple nods. Many kept the same distant, cold expression as they sat down with their families. Children seemed to be the
center of attention. An old man set his watch, glanced at the clock. One

woman in long, dark braids circled the room, examined each cluster of visitors at the benches, examined Phillip and Shelby. No one had come for her.

Phillip stood as a woman was wheeled through the door in a chair. Her skin was pale and gray, her eyes sunk in lines of wrinkles and brows, and one of her legs had been amputated at the knee. Her red pant leg was tied in a knot below. She pointed at their table, and the tall guard wheeled her over, set a brace against the rubber tire, edged back through the door, observing the other prisoners.

"Hey," said Phillip.

The woman had long, black-and-gray locks of hair pulled back behind her ears. She kept her dark eyes aimed at the table, glanced once up at Shelby.

"Hello," she said.

"This is Shelby."

The woman nodded. She looked down at her legs. "What have you brought for me?"

They listened to the buzz of voices around them. Phillip reached into his pocket, took out a chocolate bar, slid it gently across the table to the woman. She looked at it but kept her hands down at her sides, at the wheels of the chair. Her hair was slick, seemed not to have been washed in days.

"Go on," Phillip said.

When she made no further movement, he unwrapped the bar, reached to her hand, placed it between the fingers. Behind them, a child began to cry. Laughter here and there. The guards said nothing, stood together in a huddle near the door.

"How are you?" he said.

"This leg is getting me down." She took a bite of chocolate.

"I'm in school," he said. "Shelby helps me."

"He helps me too," said Shelby.

The woman nodded. "Have you found him?"

Phillip slid the cigarettes across the table. "These are for you too."

The woman picked up the carton and placed it in her lap.

"I see you took some," the woman said.

"It was a long trip."

"I asked you a question."

Phillip picked at the tabletop with his finger, drew what looked to Shelby like a face, large eyes and a thin mouth. He'd hunched his shoulders, become smaller. He circled the skull again and again. When he took his finger away, Shelby tried to find the face in the dust.

"It's hard."

"It's harder in here," said the woman. "It's been half a year and you can't do one thing I ask?"

"I made some calls. Your boyfriend was in Portland for a while. After that, I lost him."

"That does me a lot of good."

Phillip picked up the box. "I'll keep looking."

"I want a phone number."

"You'll get it."

The woman took a small bite of chocolate and looked at the clock on the wall. Shelby couldn't guess her age. She held herself old but looked younger up close. The woman's fingernails were clipped short, pointed at the tips.

"It takes an effort to come down here from the hospital," she said. "I'm in pain a lot. Next time you come, bring some news."

"I brought you something better," said Phillip.

The woman looked at the package. "Open it then," said the woman. "My hands can't fool with that paper."

Phillip tore the wrap up the side, slipped out the cardboard box. Shelby sat with hands flat on the table, watched for some expression in the woman's face but found none. When he opened the top, he took out something wrapped in paper towels. He placed it in front of his mother.

She set her hands on the towels, pulled them away. A set of binoculars, small and black, pointed up at the ceiling.

"They're used," Phillip said. "Not too strong, but you can see out your window with them. Check out the stars at night."

"How much you pay for these?" the woman said.

"Not much."

"I don't have a window," she said. "Nobody's got a window here. What do you think this is? I only get out a few hours a day."

"You can use them then."

"Blind myself looking up at the sky? You blew your money, boy."

Phillip said nothing, kept his gaze on the binoculars, which the woman had not yet touched. He seemed to slip a little in his chair, seemed to want to disappear. Behind the woman, two of the guards broke from the huddle at the door, looked past them, spread out a bit.

"He went to a lot of trouble," said Shelby, and the woman turned her eyes toward her. "You should be more thankful."

"And you should wait for an invitation. This isn't any business of yours."

The woman's eyes were direct, seemed hateful. Shelby looked away. In the silence between the three of them, they listened to the tables around them, the people. An argument, louder than theirs, had broken out in a corner, and the two guards circled toward the table, sized up the situation.

The woman lifted the binoculars, brought them to her eyes, looked up at the ceiling, the clock, then the guards. She turned the focus ring with her smallest finger, then pointed the lenses at Phillip. Shelby tried to see the woman's eyes through the lenses. The woman's teeth were yellow behind her lips.

"You've grown," she said.

In the cold and dark they made their way to the bus station, past the walls of the prison, the wire and the fencing, past the market and the stoplight. They turned left on Hawkins Street, moved from glow to glow beneath the streetlamps. Cars passed slowly on the rain-slick road. They seemed to be the only people on foot. Shelby watched her white breath cloud from under her hood, watched their reflections in puddles under the lamp glow. She reached out, took Phillip's arm, slowed him down. As they passed over each pool of water, she tried to bring herself and Phillip into focus, but they were moving too quickly, or Phillip would stamp his foot into the puddle. Circles spread from his boot step, blurred the reflections.

There was little left of the bus station, only a concrete shell and a pile of burned, broken furniture left against the side of a dumpster. The plot of land, what remained of the building, reminded Shelby of Bremerton. They seemed to be home again, but still far away. Out in the road, they could hear the rush of drain water in the gutters. Phillip pushed a cinder block over with his boot. They held hands and shivered in the dark.

Across the road was a car, parked facing the state road. Beyond it they could make the outline of the Olympics, could even smell the bay from where they stood. One of the backlights of the car flickered red, reflected against the water on the street.

They crossed the road, tried to see in through the fog. They hesitated, climbed into the backseat, shut the door behind them. It was eight o'clock.

Otis was leaning forward, against the wheel, flicking the back of the paper frog on the dash. The creature jumped at each flick, knocking against the windshield, falling on its side after. Otis set it back upright and flicked again. They listened to the tap against the glass.

Eventually, he turned, put his arm up on the seat next to him, held the frog between his fingertips. He looked at them with his two eyes, both big, one damaged.

"How'd it go?" he said.

They set their hands in their laps, looked there, listened to the rush of rainwater outside, felt a pain in their fingertips as their hands began to warm. The glow from the dashboard lit the car—the seats, the vinyl ceiling, the windows—in a dull green and white. Otis waited, looked at the frog, at the creases and folds.

"This guy didn't want to sit still," he said.

THE LOST BROTHER

I went down to the basement in late evening because of a strange, familiar shiver that frightened me. There was water down there, shin deep, and it was filled with silt and sand. My brother Albert and I had been trying to pump it out. I opened the gun cabinet and checked for his pistols, and sure enough there was one of them missing. I'd been worrying about him for a while. I'd felt something similar years before, and another feeling had set me to motion. Out from school and into home, and when I got there Ma was under the table, eating pills, talking on the phone to nobody. And another time, after a visit to my granddad—a good visit, he'd been feeling better— I woke and knew that he'd died. These were not visions to me, and not ghost whispers in my ear. I was an Atkins, and a good number of us had turned crazy over the years. But I was not yet crazy. I was fifteen and Albert's only brother, and we were friends, he and I, back then.

It was dark outside, and the moon was half, and I could see up for as many stars as I'd like. I listened to the rustle of dead leaves across the yard, and there was some smell in the air, like a storm might be moving in, though there was no other sign. I had the chills down my spine. Albert had pulled himself up on the engine of the old jeep, and he was looking down into it, like maybe he'd lost something down there. I could see the night bugs pinging against the gas lamp, and Albert's wheelchair was just outside the glow, leaned against the fender. There were other bugs—lightning—out near the river, as many as I could recall seeing that summer, and they flashed on quick and faded slow, and there was a gray mist creeping up into the yard from below. Across the water some kids were playing basketball in the dark. I couldn't see the game, but I could hear the ball and the rattle of the chain, the shouts here and there.

I went down and sat up on the engine with Albert. He was twelve years older than me and looked it that night. I cleared away some beer bottles to make a space. The oil in the pan made the air seem sweet and sharp, and I tipped the lantern in so he could see.

He was scrubbing something down there in the dark with an old toothbrush, and he was really going at it. Like he was almost there, whatever he was working on. He had two fuel pumps—one new, one old—set up on the alternator, and his black hair, pulled back and waist long, sheened in the light.

"Thought I'd surprise you," he said.

"I don't need any surprises."

He looked up at me. He had eyes the same color as his hair, and they were not yet drunk, like they usually were, this time of night.

"You're not sure what you need," he said.

Maybe that was true. He'd sensed my mood, as he often did. I was believing I needed to hold on to whatever I still had, and I told him as much.

"That's a road to ruin," he said. He was smiling. There was always something about me that he found funny.

"I could use one of those," I said.

"I've been working on a joke," he said.

"All right," I said. "I'm ready."

He handed me the new pump and turned the lantern up, traded the toothbrush for a wrench. I squinted in the brightness.

"So the farmer comes back in from the barn," he said. "And he sees all these empty bottles on the table, and one of the cowboys looks up and says to him: 'You got anything else? Seems like we're even more thirsty now.'"

I shook my head, but I laughed a little. I was nervous, I guess. "What was in the bottles?"

"I'm working on that," he said, and he caught what he was looking for with the wrench. I could hear it click into place. "You used to be the joke teller," he said.

"Those were kid's jokes."

He tensed up, trying to get the bolt loose. "Okay, old man," he said.

We got that fuel pump in there eventually. We filled the oil back up, and then I caught him under the arms and eased him down into the chair. He wheeled around in the mud and helped himself into the driver's seat. He'd done it plenty times before. The jeep was a convertible, though we didn't have the top. Most important, it had hand controls. Ma had found it somewhere in Virginia, and it had gotten Albert around enough to hold a job delivering the paper. But that hadn't lasted. There was always something breaking down.

When he turned the key it started right up. A plume of blue-white smoke blew out from the back. I took his tools down from the engine and closed the hood. It was almost ten o'clock. The headlights switched on and lit up the stretch of dead grass, and a cat who'd been watching us from the driveway flattened itself against the gravel, then just as quick disappeared into the trees.

So Albert was happy there behind the wheel, listening to the engine. Happy as I'd seen him in a while. He turned on the radio, set the seat back. The engine sounded like it was deciding between quitting and staying. I got the broom and set to sweeping out the seats. They were all full of leaves. I wondered if there might be a bird back there. I swept over and around my brother, and he was looking up at the stars.

"Why you trembling?" he said.

I looked down at him. "It's cold."

"It's not cold," he said.

In the house I got myself a jacket and packed up some food: a bag of snap beans and what was left of a pizza. I took out a half-case of beer, which seemed to me both dumb and right. I got the quilt from the couch. Then I put it all in the backseat of the jeep. I folded up Albert's chair, put that in there, and climbed in next to him.

"Where we going?" I said.

"To see my girl."

I'd tricked her name out of him the previous weekend. He'd been all secretive about her. Merrill.

"Hope she lives close," I said. "We're not going to get ten miles in this piece of shit."

He looked at me for a while, like he was maybe waiting on something else. I thought maybe I shouldn't call his jeep that. It had meant something to him. We listened to the engine idle, and I was thinking of something to say. But he reached back into the seat behind and brought up the quilt. He folded it out and set it over me.

"Hold tight of that, old man."

We went out from the city, on the state highway. There was nobody much out that night. We passed the paper mill and its ammonia smell and the stretch of farms beyond that, the bales of hay marching in rows up over the hills. In the blue they looked like a line of long, strange caterpillars to me, and the barns with their doors open like giant heads, their mouths toothless and hungry. I remembered then a broad sky, daylight, and me and Albert and Granddad stretched out in a sunflower field. We'd been in Indiana. It warmed me up a little, thinking about that, though I'd lowered my sights since then. I closed my eyes, listened to the wind, and I could picture Albert's face in that field and Granddad next to him. But I couldn't see myself. It was like it was me, but with somebody else's body, my name but somebody in my place.

"Sit up on the seat," said Albert.

I looked at him, his hair tossed every way with the wind. He looked wild and ancient to me. I had this feeling then, that there was something in the jeep that shouldn't be there. I don't know why. I got up, tossed the quilt back, sat on the back of the seat. I could see some horses behind a fence line, shadows milling about. We were going fast down the road, probably seventy-five or more, and I held on tight to the seat, bouncing a bit with the jeep. I let the wind blow my hair around, though I didn't have the length of Albert's—when I'd grown it out Ma was always yanking at it.

"Put your hands up," he said.

I did. I held them up like I was on a rollercoaster. The wind was thrumming in my ears. I looked at what I could see of the road stretched out before us, flat and straight. I couldn't make out much in the distance.

"Scream or something," said Albert. He was looking up at me, looking back at the road. He punched my leg. "You're a crazy Atkins. Act like one."

I didn't scream. I brought my hands down. We were moving fast. There was a long line of electric towers past the farms, and I watched the red lights flashing on and off. I watched and watched them till they were long past. Then I took hold of the windshield and stepped up on the dash. I set one leg over onto the hood.

Albert grabbed hold of my other leg. "What the hell are you doing?"

The wind was all in my face. "Let go," I said.

"Get back in here."

"I'm going to fall," I said.

"Daniel," he said. He was shouting at me.

"I'm going to fall if you slow down."

He couldn't do that though. He had one hand on my leg, one on the steering wheel.

"I'm falling Albert," I said.

He let go of my leg and put his hand on the brake switch, though he didn't pull on it. I climbed out onto the hood and held onto the windshield, my back toward the road. We were flying down the road. My jacket was filled up with air, like it might lift me away, and what hair I had was in my eyes. I looked at Albert through the glass.

"I'm crazier than hell," I said. I had to yell it above the wind.

"Don't let go," he said.

"I won't. You want me to scream?"

We hit a dip in the road, and I lost my footing for a second. When I looked down I was crushing one of the windshield wipers with my shoe.

"Don't let go," he said.

"You want me to scream?"

"Whatever you want. Don't let go."

I screamed. I screamed as loud as I could. I took my foot off the wiper and set it on the hood again. I could feel the metal popping under my weight and the cold of the wind all down my spine. The farmland was flying past us. I screamed some more and looked back on the road. There was a car back there, way back. The headlights seemed like one headlight. I held one of my fists in the air.

"Don't slow down," I shouted at Albert.

"I won't," he said. "Get your hand back down."

So I did that. I wasn't scared at all. I wanted to dance up there on the hood.

"How crazy are you?" said Albert.

"Crazier than hell."

"Everybody knows that."

"Damn straight they know."

"Tell them," he said.

"I'm crazy," I yelled out. "I'm crazier than hell."

"Nobody crazier," he said. "Now get back in here."

I looked behind me, into the wind. It about lifted me off of there. I watched the tobacco fields coming toward us in the dark.

"I can't ever fall," I shouted at Albert.

"That's right, don't do that."

I looked at him through the glass again. "I'm not ever going to."

"Okay," he said. "I hear you."

I looked as clear at him through that glass as I could manage. We hit another dip in the road, and my feet came off the hood for just a second. I grabbed onto the busted wiper.

"You can slow down then," I said.

And when he did, I climbed back over the windshield and into the seat. The car behind us passed us on the left side and we watched it go, an old drunk farmer it looked like. I took up the quilt again. I hadn't lost the shivers.

"Where's she live?" I said.

"Farther on."

"Near Jake?"

"No."

And he didn't say anything more. He'd been in the Gulf War, Albert, and I thought maybe we might see one of his friends tonight. They were scattered all about these parts. I came up every weekend from Raleigh on the bus, spent Friday and Saturday nights with him. With his veteran's check we bought groceries for the week, worked on the car. Whatever there was to do. We had a canoe, and we'd take that out in the river when we felt like it, if the water was still enough to get back upstream. We read the newspaper to each other. We watched TV. We drank. In the spring and summers we had a vegetable garden, though we didn't have much success with that. We went bowling sometimes. Albert had been a combat engineer in the war. They found and disabled landmines. They called themselves a name that I'd always liked. Sappers. He'd had a friend who missed a wire. The man's helmet snapped Albert's spine. I'd heard this story only a few times. There was a pop and then the other pop and then silence. Stateside, I'd lived with him for a while in the hospital, sneaking around, after Ma went under the table.

"How about some beers?" said Albert.

I reached back, pulled two from the twelve. I opened them, passed one over.

He took a long swig and then another. He looked out on the road for a while and we didn't say anything. We watched the farmhouses spaced every few miles, some standing, some fallen, some looking to. I drank my beer. I didn't want the cold of the drink, but I kept sipping at it. About the time it was empty Albert turned to look at me.

"That was fun as hell," he said.

I was feeling the buzz already. "Damn right. That was fun as all get out."

"You're not that crazy," he said.

"No," I said. "That was above me."

"No need to do that again."

"No," I said. "That's it for now."

We took a turnoff from the highway and drove along next to a long gully filled with dark water. The moon had reached its height and was beginning to dip, and I watched it, the strange patches of gray and blue. I tried to see a face in the moon, but I couldn't quite make it out. That storm smell was in the air again, and there were clouds off toward the north, not dark but white-gray, and I watched them, waiting for lightning. The road turned to gravel and we slowed down. We could hear the rocks and pebbles kick up from the tires, clattering in the wheel wells and popping against the chassis. I took out the beans as we rode along and snapped a few in half, chewed them down. I handed a couple to Albert, and he studied them, set them on the dashboard. I watched them rattle with the movement of the jeep till they became lodged against the windshield. I pulled my hands from beneath the quilt. Unsteady. I was still trembling. They looked like mad hands to me.

We pulled into a trailer park, and a couple dogs came out and chased along beside us. We passed empty clotheslines and a yard full of tires and bicycles. An old metal barrel filled with wood, burn marks down the side. Lights inside the trailers were blue and shifting, televisions likely, but maybe ghosts, said Albert, and he made some creepy voice and I rolled my eyes. I wasn't sure how, but he was making fun of me. There were chairs tossed here and there, sideways, like no one would be sitting out soon, and the dogs gave up as we pulled past a small lake in which I could see the moon, and at the near end I could make out a school bus, half sunk in the dark water. I curled my hands into fists, thought that might help some. We pulled up next to a yellow trailer with Christmas lights—white, red, and green—though it was the wrong season. They were strung all along the roof and around the windows.

When Albert cut the engine we could hear some music from the inside, something slow and strange, and beyond that the crickets ticking together out by the lake. He switched off the headlights and we sat and listened to the music. We finished our beers—my second, Albert's third—and watched for movement in the trailer. I put my fingers up to my neck, to feel my pulse and what my heart was pushing through.

A light came on above us, and we both held our hands up to block the shine. In that light Albert looked as old as I'd ever seen him. He looked as old as Ma. Older.

Somebody came out on the steps, and Albert reached over and opened the glove box, and there in the light I could see one of his pistols. The one missing from the gun cabinet. The long black handle was sticking out from the papers and maps. But he left the pistol there and took out a roll of money. He closed the box and I got out and got his chair.

Merrill came down the steps. She was wearing a black dress and a thin rope necklace, and boots. When I'd gotten Albert out of the jeep and settled into his chair, she took his head in her hands, gentle, like she was trying to find his ears in all that hair of his. We were just outside the light, but I could see that she was a little older than Albert. Her hair was tied back with a band and she had a slight smile, though it seemed to me that there was maybe another face behind the first, one that was sad and not smiling. She bent down and kissed him at the bridge of his nose, and then she just held his head for a while, but she was looking over at me.

"Daniel," I said, though she hadn't asked.

"The brother," she said.

"I told you I would," said Albert.

She nodded and took her hands from his head, slowly, like maybe she might put them back there again.

"Can I touch you?" she said.

I looked at Albert, and he just shrugged. I felt like there was maybe a joke being put on me.

"Where?" I said.

She smiled. "Right here."

I shrugged. "All right."

She stepped over and put one of her boots on my shoe, then she pushed back my hair with the tips of her fingers. I looked away.

"Can I turn you into the light?" she said.

"Not too much," I said.

"Just a little."

When she turned me, she pushed my hair back again and lifted my chin up. I had to squint in the brightness.

"You all right?" she said.

"It's strange," I said.

"You're shaking."

"I'm cold."

"You don't feel cold," she said. "You're a beautiful child."

"I'm not a child."

"No," she said.

I wanted to get out of that light then, and maybe she sensed this, because she took me out. She let go of me.

"Let's say we go inside," she said.

So we went up into the trailer. I leaned Albert and his chair back and pulled him up the steps. I'd done this many places before. I knew the trick of it. He stared up at me.

"You're spooking," he said.

"Says you."

There was a couch inside, two chairs, lampshades. Drapes on the windows. Merrill turned off the spotlight outside, and there was a white candle on a small table, lit, and the red and green lights shining through the glass. I liked the music on the radio. Still slow, but no longer strange. Something familiar, though I could not quite place it. Merrill was in the kitchen, and her steps seemed to follow the music as she walked about. A big map of the country was pinned up on the wall opposite the couch, and I examined it for a moment. Little stars drawn here and there: Fresno and Grand Junction, Boston and Sioux Falls, Portland, both of them. Below, on a shelf, were about a dozen porcelain mice, each of them the same it seemed. Each of them standing with the same hopeful expression—big eyes—but dressed different, in little felt outfits. A hippie and a surgeon, a nurse and a fisherman. One of them held a butterfly net.

Merrill called from the kitchen. "Don't make fun of my mice, Daniel Atkins."

"I thought they were rats," I said.

She looked at me from over the counter. "You can wait outside in the jeep if you want."

I looked at Albert, and he gave me a look I couldn't read. He took a swig off a beer.

"I didn't mean nothing by it," I said.

"Then have a seat," she said.

I sat down in a chair next to Albert, and he closed his eyes and listened to the music. He started moving his shoulders, his neck. He seemed to be whispering some words, though there weren't any voices on the radio. I crossed my arms over my chest. I was shivering something terrible.

"I've got a whole box of donuts here," said Merrill. "I think these are going to be good. You'll have some donuts?"

"Sure," said Albert. He opened his eyes then and reached into his pocket. He took out the roll of money—twenties—and handed it to me. He nodded at Merrill.

"Give it to her?" I said.

He nodded.

So I got up and leaned over the counter. I looked at her for a moment. I was scared of her, though I didn't want to show it. I handed over the money.

"Those are steep donuts," I said.

Something young came over her face then. Some sort of pleasant tremor it seemed to me. She had the same expression as when she'd tipped me into the light. She reached toward the money but took hold of my wrist. Her grip was tight, and I didn't know if I could pull free.

"Did you hear that, Albert?" she said.

He was laughing. "I heard him."

"Steep donuts."

"You sending him out?" said Albert.

She was laughing now, and she began to move again to the music. "I was never to send Daniel Atkins out," she said.

And then she put the money away and let go of me. She handed over the donuts.

So, we had some donuts and some beer, and I was feeling all right. Merrill helped my brother out of his chair, helped set him on the couch. She leaned him back till his head was lying on a pillow. Then she slipped his shirt off, turned him over. In the hospitals I'd seen the nurses do this a hundred times. He had his eyes closed, and it seemed that his face held some troubled thought. I could barely make it out in the candlelight. It sent a chill down my shoulders. He reached back, and she took his hand.

"There's a blanket," said Merrill. "On the bed in the room. When you get it, bring me the brush on the nightstand."

"Me?" I said.

"Yes you, Daniel Atkins."

So I went in there and got the blanket. And I got the brush. On the stand there was a picture of two teenagers. One was spot-on for Merrill, and she and a boy were leaning against a fence. The boy she was with was good-looking, and he held an old-time pocket watch in his open palm. He was looking at that watch like it was the most curious thing. The younger Merrill looked delighted. I picked up the picture and checked the hallway. I studied that watch in the picture. I was wondering what was so curious about it. I wondered if the boy was just performing for the camera. I was getting pretty drunk. A minute, and I set the picture back as best as I could.

In the den I gave Merrill the brush, and she looked at the blanket and said, "Go on." So I sat back in the chair and pulled the blanket over me. I took the last swig of a beer and put my feet up on the table.

"Where do you live during the week?" said Merrill.

"Me?" I said.

"Yes you. I don't want to talk to this fool brother of yours."

"Hey," said Albert.

"Hey," said Merrill.

"With my Ma," I said. "Up in Raleigh."

"Are you in high school yet?"

"Next year," I said. "If some things start to go right. I've missed some time lately."

She nodded. "We've all got things to take care of. Albert has told me some about you."

"A little," said Albert.

"What does he say?" I said.

Merrill was sitting next to him, and she poured some clear, scented oil onto her hands. Then she rubbed it into Albert's back. "You're a hell of a bowler," she said. "That's him talking. What else? Bowling's a good start. Someone takes something up, they should be good at it. You're a swimmer, and you work nights at a restaurant. Dishes, right?"

"Boring," I said.

She rubbed the oil into his shoulders, down his spine. "Well he didn't tell me that part. Here's one. You order your clothes on hangers, light to dark."

I smiled at that. "Which way?"

She considered. "Light on the left."

"Wrong."

"I've got to keep closer attention," she said. "Now I've got to make up for it. When you were younger you had a duck who you thought was your girlfriend."

I sat up at that. I looked at my brother. "Albert!" I said.

He opened his eyes and looked up at me. They were both laughing.

"Be careful what you ask," said Merrill.

I tucked the blanket up to my neck. "She was just my friend."

And that set them to laughing more. I let them ride that out. I wasn't going to say another word. I looked over at the mice, and for some reason I started thinking about that picture in Merrill's room. I listened to the music, and I was buzzing pretty good. I thought I might just close my eyes if I could get warm enough.

"I had a mule when I was a kid," said Merrill. "An old blind mule. His name was Albert."

"No it wasn't," said Albert.

"Think what you like," she said. "But I used to take care of him. He'd follow me around in the fields. We were picking apples. And he'd eat the hell out of those apples. I'd have to keep them from him, or else he'd get sick if he ate too many. I had him for years. When I first got him they were like 'he won't last a year,' but he just went on and on."

"What was his real name?" I said.

"Oh, I don't know. What was your duck's name?"

I didn't say anything.

"Good," she said. "That's yours to keep."

She took up the brush then, and she took up Albert's hair and began pulling it back. She worked out the tangles. He curled his arm under his cheek.

She brushed his hair straight. She hummed to the radio while she was working, and I watched her. She took a lot of care with it, I thought. I was about ready to close my eyes.

When she was done with the brush, she reached over to a drawer and took out a pair of scissors. She ran her thumb down the blade.

"You sure about this?" she said.

"Yes," said Albert, a whisper.

I sat up from the chair. "No."

Albert opened one eye and looked at me. "I've been thinking about it. This isn't spur of the moment."

"It'll take you years to grow back," I said.

"It's time to let go of things," he said.

He closed the eye and set his head against the pillow. Merrill watched me for a while, and then she slipped some hair between her fingers and cut off a few strands. She set them across his face.

"Last chance," she said.

"I told you," Albert said.

She looked at me and waited. She snipped the scissors a few times in the air, waited for something from either of us. I was drunk. I looked over at Albert, and he didn't move. I decided I wouldn't say anything else. He seemed to me at peace there, as much as I'd seen him. Merrill moved to the music again, and she began to cut his hair. "It's a long, long way to the moon," she sang, though there weren't any voices on the radio.

Merrill brought the candle over and pulled a chair up next to me. She had Albert's hair in her fist, and we sat there for a while and watched him sleep. His face was slack and silent, and it seemed to me that he was without dreams. It put me in mind of my grandfather again, and I could see us—me, Granddad, and Albert—years before, down in the sunflowers in Indiana. There were grasshoppers popping over us. Just a few at first, then more, then a hundred it seemed. Like they'd arrived just behind us. We were picking them off our shirts, or we'd flick them at each other, and they'd leave some spit behind. There wasn't any shade, and the sun was warm and it dried our clothes. We'd been caught out in the rain, in the back of a stranger's pickup that morning. We were on our way to St. Louis, to see about a basketball scholarship for Albert, though that hadn't worked out. We could just reach up and grab as many grasshoppers as we liked. They'd sit on the tips of your fingers if you let them, their legs poking at you. I caught the most, and Granddad looked at my hands and said, "These flowers'll be gone in a week now."

Merrill had brought out some spools of thread, and she set those on the table between us. She had a needle between her teeth, and she was digging around in a sewing kit for something.

"Would you hold this for me?" she said, a mumble.

I took Albert's hair. I held it tight so it wouldn't slip out of my hand. It was soft and heavy and I brought it down near the candlelight. There were all different colors in there. Black mostly, but auburn and even some gray. Brown hair, like mine, but I'd never seen it before in Albert's. It seemed like it might be a few people's hair, all mixed together.

Merrill found what she was looking for, and I handed the hair back. She made a knot of it at the end, held it together that way. I still had some strands stuck to my fist, and I took those and set them on my knee. She threaded the needle in the candlelight.

"What happened to your duck?" she said.

I shrugged. "Christmas dinner."

She looked over at me. "You're lying."

"Maybe."

"You got another girl now?"

"Maybe," I said.

"Well, you either do or you don't."

"I don't I guess."

Merrill got that needle threaded. "You got your eye on one?"

"Maybe."

"I know parrots that have more words than you," she said.

"I guess."

She smiled a little, set a fancy clip on Albert's hair. She started sewing the knot to the clip. "What's her name?"

"Amy."

"That's a pretty name," she said.

"I made it up."

I tried to take deep breaths. I was trying to get warmer. I looked around the room. There wasn't much to it. Just the furniture, a TV. The mice. I looked up at the map on the wall.

"You been to those places you marked?" I said.

"When I was younger."

"What were they like?"

She considered that, though she didn't take her eyes from what she was doing. "They weren't too good I guess."

"Did you get those mice there?"

"No."

"Did you make those little outfits for them?"

"I know better than to answer that," she said. She pulled the thread tight. "You're getting ahead with your questions. Time for me to ask one."

"All right."

"Go get us some beers first."

"Was that a statement or a question?"

"That was a statement," she said. "And yours was a question. So now you're down two."

I got up and got the beers. When I settled back I nodded at the hair. "What are you making?"

"Not your turn," Merrill said. "What's your mom like?"

"She's tall."

"Tall huh? She look like you?"

"A little."

"What does she do?"

I shrugged. "Albert's told you about her."

"No," she said. "He hasn't."

I thought about Ma. I tried to picture her in my mind. "She takes care of herself. She's getting better at that. She tries to stay in this world as much as she can."

"And you're close to her?"

"No," I said. "She's not someone to get close to. That's not in her. But I spend a lot of time with her. Weekends she's at her sister's. My turn?"

Merrill finished a stitch in the clip, took up the scissors. "Okay."

"You got other boyfriends besides Albert?"

She nodded. "I do."

"What are their names?"

"A name is a powerful thing," she said.

"One of them then."

She thought about that. She looked up at the map. "Hank."

"Did you make that up?"

"Yes," she said. "My turn. Why are you shivering all the time?"

"Cause I'm drinking cold beer."

"Is that it?"

"I guess."

"You ever kissed a girl?"

I pulled down the blanket a bit. I didn't like that question much, but I didn't want to show it. I thought about it awhile, though there wasn't much to think on.

"No," I said.

"Why not?"

"I suppose the opportunity hasn't come along."

"I doubt that," she said. "Do you want to kiss me?"

I thought about that, and there was plenty to think on. "I guess not."

"Why not?"

I blinked. "Because you're my brother's girlfriend."

"He said it'd be all right."

I looked over at my brother. "Did he?"

"Yes," she said. "And it would quit you of your shivers."

"Is that right?" I said. "You got magic lips?"

"That's right. Magic lips," she said. She pulled another stitch tight but didn't cut it yet. She looked over at me. "I'm going to ask you again, and that's going to be the last time. You're not going to get this kind of courtesy from other women. You understand?"

"Maybe I should take some notes."

"Maybe," she said. "Would you like to kiss me?"

I thought about that. "All right."

"Well," she said. "I don't think so. You had your chance."

I settled back in the chair. I pulled the blanket up. I wanted to pull it over my head.

She set the hair aside and got up and leaned over me. "I don't want you to touch me this time, all right?"

"Okay," I said.

She kissed me then. She turned her head to the side and ran her fingers at the back of my scalp. "Close your eyes, dummy," she said.

So I closed my eyes, and she kissed me some more. She pinched one of my ears with a fingernail and pushed my head back against the chair. I could feel her weight against my knees. I listened to the music and felt her sway with and, it seemed to me, within it. She pulled my lip with her teeth, and her kiss was warm and it made me warm. I leaned forward in the chair. We were done before I wanted us to be. She sat back and took up Albert's hair again.

"Don't say anything," she said.

"Okay."

"Some day you'll figure what to say after, but it's got to be the right thing. If you don't know, then keep quiet. Got it?"

I closed my eyes. "This is complicated."

"No it's not," she said. "Can I ask you something?"

"Sure."

"Did you see that picture in my room?"

I opened my eyes again. "I think you put it out there for me to see."

She nodded. "Well bully for you. I did. I was scared of you coming here tonight."

"Why?"

"That's my brother in the picture. He and I were close once. That's a picture I had that'd fit the frame."

"He's older than that now," I said.

"He died when he was eighteen," she said. "He was working a ferry in the Pamlico. He tried to jump from the dock in a storm. He hit his head and went straight down. I miss him a lot. He and I were as close as you and Albert."

I didn't say anything to that.

"You remind me of him," she said.

"I do?"

"Well, I suppose if you had three eyes you'd still remind me of him."

"What do you mean?"

She didn't say anything.

I thought about something. I thought it through twice before I said it. "Did you teach him how to kiss?"

"My brother?" she said.

"Yes."

She laughed a little at that. She didn't take her eyes from the stitching. "No," she said. "But I guess you won't believe me."

"I believe you," I said.

"You want to know his name?"

"Yes," I said.

She studied me for a moment. I couldn't read her face in the candle-light. She set the hair aside. Then she leaned over to my ear and whispered his name.

We went out back, the three of us. A big stretch of clouds had moved in, and the stars were all gone. There was lightning in the distance, and the clouds would flash up every minute or so, dull and sudden. A warm breeze from the north pushed across the lake. We took Albert down to the water's edge. He was wide-awake now, though he was yawning. He couldn't seem to stop. His eyes were all wet, and it was like I couldn't recognize him with all that hair gone. He looked like something young had come over him. There were frogs making all kinds of sounds—low then high—along the shore. "Peepers," Merrill said to us, nodding out into the dark. We got Albert down there, then we pushed his chair a ways into the water. Not too far. It sent a couple ducks flying out from the reeds, honking and complaining. We watched them skim across the water and then disappear into a mist in the center of the lake.

We got Albert a beer and a donut. "This water's cold," he said. But it wasn't all that cold. Me and Merrill stripped down to our underwear, and we waded out into the water, the scum and rocks against our feet.

"There's brambles in here," she said. "Watch where you go."

I went under and I couldn't see anything, but as I settled I could hear the blood in my head, bouncing through the water it seemed. I was warm down there. I came up and wiped my eyes. I let my sight adjust. I looked back toward Albert. I was about twenty yards out into the water, and he pointed over and past me with his beer.

"What's that out there?" he said.

I turned where he was looking, and I saw the school bus. I waited for the next flash of lightning.

"That's been there for years," said Merrill.

"How'd it get there?"

"Somebody was very drunk, I suppose."

When the lightning came I could see that all the windows were smashed out. Cattails were growing all around it, and it rested low against the bank. Somebody had popped the tires a long time ago.

"How come no one's pulled it out?" I said.

"It's junk," said Merrill. "I know what you're thinking. There's no kids in there."

"How do you know?"

"You're spooking again," said Albert.

And I was. I didn't like that bus in there. There were all sorts of things floating around my legs. I'd swallowed some water.

"I want to get out there with you," said Albert.

I looked at him. "Out in the water?"

"Hell yeah, out in the water. I never get to do anything fun."

He dropped his bottle in the water and took off his shirt again. We swam up to him. I got him under an arm and Merrill got him under the other arm, and we eased him out of the chair and turned him. He settled back with us, and he tensed a bit as he went into the water. His face was pointing up at the clouds. The darkness of the water was bobbing at his neck. "That's good," he said. I had my arm across his chest, my ribs at his back. Merrill took him from the other side.

"Don't let go now," said Albert.

"No," we said.

"I'll drop for sure."

"We won't," we said.

"Then go out some."

We pushed past the reeds, and out a little ways from shore, out where the water was colder. We moved away from the bus, and I was glad of that. And then I got to thinking about Merrill's brother and how he'd drowned. We went out a ways more, till I couldn't feel the mud at my feet. We paddled out farther. I looked over at her.

"You all right with this?" I said. I couldn't see much of her face in the dark. Our chins were dipping under, and we could hear thunder off in the distance.

"She's all right," said Albert.

"I can take the weight," said Merrill.

We went out toward the mist, and the water became very cold. I set my hip against Albert to keep him up. It took me and Merrill awhile to keep our legs from tangling, but we got the trick of it.

The air smelled flat and green, and we could hear the night bugs and the peepers chirping all along the shore. I looked out toward the mist. It was not much farther out now. I thought we might could make it there and then turn back. I was feeling all right. I felt like I could take my brother across the ocean if it needed doing. And I was glad to have Merrill there with us. It seemed to me like we were the only three people left in the world. Like all but near us was empty space. I looked at the two of them in the flash of lightning.

"Daniel," said Albert. He had his eyes closed. He was just a face and two shoulders in the water. "Do you remember a scarecrow?"

I kicked under the water. "No."

"Ma's," he said.

"No."

"I told you about it though."

"No," I said. "I don't know anything about that."

There was another flash of lightning, close, I thought, and I said so. We listened to the thunder after.

"It ain't that close," said Albert. Then he looked over at Merrill. "Did I tell you?"

"What?"

"The scarecrow."

"I don't think so," she said.

"I'm drunk," he said. "It was somebody close to me, but I can't remember now."

"Who?" I said.

"The person I told."

"Well tell us."

"There's nothing to tell," he said.

"We're going to dunk you under."

He laughed at that, clutched onto my arm. "Don't."

"Tell it," I said. "Then we'll turn around."

We were into the mist now, and the air was warmer, though I could hear a breeze moving up along the shore and through the fields. I took a tighter grip across my brother's chest.

"It had a face of corn," he said. "She had this box for a head. The scarecrow I mean. It was just a couple sticks and some old clothes, and the box for a head, and Ma spent all night at the table, gluing this corn to the box. She made the eyes and a mouth. I don't know. She just put the corn all over the head. Different shades of corn. She stayed up like she would. No sleep. Just gluing this face on the box. A kernel at a time."

"Why'd she do that?" said Merrill.

"Cause she's crazier than hell," said Albert.

I laughed. "She's crazier than all get out."

But Albert wasn't laughing. "You know what happened."

"What happened?" I said.

He reached up and swatted at the mist. "I can't see the sky through all this," he said. "We could be under the water for all I knew. The birds came and ate all the corn off. It was gone by the afternoon. There was so many of them, they ripped the box right off the sticks. You could see them out there fighting over the head."

I thought it might be good to turn back now. I started to turn us, but they wouldn't come.

"My mom had a garden just like that," said Merrill.

"We're not talking about your mom," said Albert.

"What are we talking about then?"

"I didn't say anything about any fucking garden. Why don't you listen?"

"You're drunk," I said.

"So?"

"So, you're being rude."

"I'm trying to tell a fucking story, but I've lost it now."

"Sorry," said Merrill.

"Drop me if you want," he said.

"No one said anything about dropping you," she said.

"I can get drunk if I want. I've been through enough."

"Nobody said you haven't," she said.

"I haven't been through shit," he said.

He laughed, and I had this feeling he was going to try to slip from us then. I thought about how crazy a drowning person can get.

"Let's go back," I said.

"You hear that wind?" he said.

We listened, and it was thunder we heard, from the west, not the north. When it faded I listened to the trees, and sure enough there was a wind coming down on us. I could feel my legs starting to cramp up.

"Why'd y'all bring me out in the water?" said Albert. "It's lightning out."

I looked around, and the mist was spinning in every direction with the wind. I held tight to Albert, and I turned us around. I pulled hard. We could see the rain off in the distance. A gray it seemed against the blue.

"Y'all are stupid," said Albert.

"You're stupid," Merrill said.

"What was in your garden?"

"There wasn't anything in there," she said.

"Did y'all have corn?" he said.

"Snap at me," she said.

The shore seemed like a long ways off. I was thinking of pulling Merrill's hand away. I thought I'd take hold of my brother and make some time.

"Man, did y'all have corn or not?" he said.

"Yes," said Merrill.

"What kind?"

"Why you asking?"

"It's important to me," he said.

"Well, I don't remember."

He settled back then. He'd been all tight. There was a lightning flash, and I could see that school bus then. I was glad to see it now. I made for that end of shore.

"It don't matter I guess," he said. He closed his eyes and set his head back in the water. "Can y'all hear that wind?"

We said we could. We could hardly hear anything else by then.

"I once had a friend blown right off the road."

"By the wind?" said Merrill.

"No," he said.

I drove on the way back. It was just the two of us. I wasn't going to let him behind the wheel. We had no top for the jeep. The rain was coming down not straight but sideways with the wind, and I was soaking wet and had to wipe the water from my eyes. We listened to it fall, slap against the pavement, and tin-tap against the jeep. The wiper I'd busted on the passenger side didn't work, and we went slow down into the dark. I was feeling sober and feeling bad. The rain and the swim had sobered me up. I was getting a feeling then, but I couldn't place it. Albert sat next to me holding his hair in his hand, running his fingers through it.

"I wanted you to have this," he said.

"I didn't ask for it."

"I know," he said. "I was hoping you'd clip it on and feel it behind you."

I didn't say anything to that.

"It's all wet now."

"That's all right," I said. "I'm going to grow mine out. We got the same length now. We'll have us a race with it. Down to our butts."

"First one gets this jeep," he said.

I looked at him. "This is yours."

"That's the deal," he said. "Can't have a race without a bet."

"All right," I said.

Albert looked down at his chest. "Your butt's closer to your head than mine is."

"I guess."

"I'm getting screwed."

We drove on for a while, and I kept watch at what the headlights would show. We listened to the thunder, and the lightning turned the road like day in front of us. We passed those horses behind the fence, and they were all worked up with the storm. Milling about the field, some were shaking their heads. They kind of looked like they were ready to break loose. I wiped the rain from my eyes.

"Why're you shaking?" he said.

"It's cold out."

"It's not that cold," he said. "You've been shaking all night." He looked in the back seat. "Where's the quilt?"

"We left it at Merrill's," I said. "You were the one that wanted to go."

He looked out into the dark. His clothes were all soaked through.

"Why you climbing on hoods and shit?" he said. "That was damn stupid."

"I couldn't help it," I said.

"That's bullshit. That's something Ma would say. I got no one to rely on but you. Understand? Look at me. I'm all fucked up."

"You're not all fucked up," I said.

He held up his hair, studying it. It seemed like it was the first time he'd seen it.

"You're not like you used to be," he said.

He kept looking at the hair in his hand. He played for a while with the clip that Merrill had sewn on. We were moving past the farmhouses now, and he looked out at them, out at the rain. Then he reached back and tossed his hair out into the dark.

I pulled on the brake switch and pulled the jeep over to the shoulder. I had to take it slow because of the rain. When we came to a stop I put the switch into Park. We sat there in the rain for a while.

"Go get it," I said.

"I can't fucking walk. You go get it."

"It's your hair," I said.

"It's your hair," he said. "Leave it there if you want."

I took the key out of the ignition and got out. "Don't go anywhere."

"Where am I to go?" he said.

I left the headlights on and went back on the road. I couldn't hardly see anything in the rain. There were some shapes: the fence line down below the hill, a long stretch of tree line that we'd passed. I tried to figure how far we'd gone. I searched all down the shoulder of the road, waiting for the lightning to see anything. There were some old tire treads, an old shirt. Some bottles and a ball of aluminum foil. I walked along for a while, and then I walked some more. A car came up toward me, and I looked back to the jeep. I could barely make out the red lights in all that rain, and the car went on by. I walked a ways past where Albert had thrown the hair. I'd thought all night that I was moving into crazy. I thought the shivers might be a sign of it. Part of me wanted it to come on. I was hoping to trade it for lonely.

There was a farmhouse off in the fields, and I recognized it I thought. I thought maybe we'd just passed it before he threw his hair out. They all looked alike. I headed back. I looked along in the mud and peered down the slope. If it'd gone that far, I wouldn't find it tonight. Another car was rushing down the road, and I waited for the headlights. I looked down at my feet, holding my hand up to shield my eyes from the rain. I reached down and took hold. It was then I heard the gunshot. I thought at first it was thunder, but it had come from the jeep. The car went rushing by.

I looked up, and I couldn't see much in the rain, just that car trailing off toward the jeep. I took off running. I was a long ways it seemed. The car passed my brother's jeep and kept going. I ran past all the trash I'd seen, all the farmhouses. A flash of lightning lit up the road, and I kept running. I ran as fast as I ever did. When I closed the distance some I could see him up there, his head leaned back in the seat. I ran through the rain.

When I got up to him, the pistol was in his lap. He was looking up into the rain.

"Sorry," he said.

"Are you hit?"

He looked down at his body. "I guess not," he said.

I took up the pistol and threw it out into the fields. It disappeared into the dark and the rain.

"That was my best pistol," he said.

"Tough shit."

"I brought that back with me. It belonged to my friend."

I looked at him. I kicked the side of the jeep. "I don't want to hear about your fucking friend."

I walked around for a while, on the shoulder of the road. Up then back, and I wouldn't look at my brother. The rain came down on me. There was a farmhouse across the field, and I could see a man standing there. On the porch, standing in shadow. He had his hands in his pockets and was looking out across the way.

It was necessary to hold on to what I still had. This is what I would've told that man. I wouldn't have meant Albert or Ma, though I wanted to hold on to them. I'd have meant my head. The insides. I wanted to hold on to my insides. I wondered if there was any hope in it. I walked around in the headlights so maybe the man or Albert could take a good look at me.

I went and checked on my brother. He was dripping wet, and in his face I could see my mom. His hair was all short, stuck to his head.

"Are you going to hit me?" he said.

"I'm thinking it."

"Don't fuck up my nose," he said. I didn't say anything to that. I wasn't going to hit Albert. I stood there in the rain and watched him. I was waiting on something I suppose. Though I felt like it was on me. I wiped the rain from my eyes, and I dropped his hair into his lap. We both looked down at it. We couldn't see any colors but dark in it. He sat and I stood. In the rain we studied that hair. I was young back then. And I was hoping maybe he could help me out.

THIEVES I'VE KNOWN

A boxer's offense is designed to create openings in the opponent's defense and to land blows to the vulnerable points of the head and body from the waist up. Power originates as she pushes off from her feet; its degree depends upon her ability to link the muscles of the legs, the back, the shoulders, and the arms into a chain of force. A boxer's attack consists of such basic blows as left jab, right cross, left hook, and uppercut.

Helen, fifteen, throws a hook from her left foot, covers her midsection, ducks, takes a hit on her padded headgear, feints with the left again, listens to her trainer's voice, mumbled through his mouthpiece: move back and back in, keep me in the center, I'll kill you near the ropes. Move with your feet, keep your waist straight. Next time you lean back, I'll knock you down; and when she does lean back, he does knock her down, with a strong hook to her forehead and a sudden shove of hips. After the fall, she stares at the tubes of fluorescent lights above the gym, the glow of the streetlamp through the windows, the nightbugs outside. She presses her gloves against the canvas, feels the cold lick of sweat against her T-shirt.

I haven't started the count yet, he says. Not even in the corner yet. You wait till five before you get up. Think about where you are, and think about what put you there. Three. You know I'll push hard now. I'm going to see what you've got left. Five.

Helen stands, punches her gloves together, hops on her toes. He is a head taller than her, wider in the chest and waist, with longer arms and better technique. Dark hair covers his chest and shoulders. He moves in and she sidesteps, takes another jab to the head but slips in one of her own. He chooses not to cover, tries a jab and misses. She has already turned, gives him a hard shot to the ribs and then a harder one still with the other arm. Before he can wrap her up, she steps away, covers her head as she was taught, swings to the center of the ring. She hears the slap of her punches only now, seconds after they landed. Because she holds her ground, he tries a cross and it glances off the top of her skull, but he pays with two blows to his ribs, the other side this time. He steps away and circles the ring, keeps a distance from her. He notes that she has been practicing.

I'm going to knock you down now, he says, and again, he does. A flurry of hooks and crosses, most of them missing. She plants a strong jab in his gut, hears nothing, moves back, which was the mistake: he connects to the side of her head and then with the right square to the nose, her headgear saving the bone from cracking. It's only after she falls, after her feet fly from the canvas, her back slapping flat against the mat, that she hears his grunt of surprise. Not now, but from seconds before, the jab to the gut. She looks at the fluorescent lights again. She tastes the blood in her mouthpiece as he retires to the corner.

I haven't started yet, he says. The words come out without vowels. Helen shakes her head, sits up but does not rise. Two, he says. You've got me thinking now. Got me thinking this'll go an extra round. I'm not going to push it hard this time, or maybe I will. But if I'm smart I won't. Five. Stay down. I'm thinking I might not bring all I got here. So what are you going to do?

Keep you moving, she says. I'm going to move around.

Get up now, he says. And make sure you do that.

On the train, Omar, twelve, finds it hard to understand the mumbled voice of the conductor who announces the station stops. He likes to talk to his mother on the train, though she doesn't ride with him; it keeps people away. He thinks about his brother and the belt. A woman with a baby sits across from him, and a man dressed in two heavy coats. Give me your belt, his brother had said to him through the broken glass of the warehouse window. What do you want my belt for? Just give it here. So, Omar had handed it over and watched as his brother wrapped it around his arm. The boy took out a needle from his sock.

His brother often talked as he was shooting up. Mama's too fat, his brother had said. She eats too much.

When he was younger, when he'd handed the belt over, Omar hoped he'd always live with his mother, thought about no matter how old he became, the three of them would still live in the same house. I don't want no skinny-bones mama, he'd said. She isn't a girl. I don't want to sit on the lap of no skinny-bones girl.

He takes the steps from the subway station two at a time, watches his frost breath as he comes above ground. The abandoned car in the lot near the station has a cracked windshield with blood and a few strands of hair, and in a lot not unlike this one, a month before, two kids were trapped in an abandoned refrigerator, suffocated. Omar likes the tug-boats in the harbor, he can see their red running lights from the top floor of his apartment building, but to get there—to the top floor—he has to pass the steps on the sixteenth, the hallway with no lightbulbs, where, often enough, he can hear a man crying. But Omar has never seen this man, thinks he might be an old man, by the sound of the voice, takes the steps one at a time when he passes.

If he sits on the rooftop—his legs hanging over the side—at sunset, Omar can see the rats emerge from the riverbank. They look like an army of insects from where he sits. They cross the lot where the car with the cracked windshield sits, they pass over the rolls of carpets, the broken chairs and the trash and the abandoned tires.

It's the last day of the month, this day, and Omar passes his own apartment building, passes the cemetery with the broken headstones— no one has been buried there for years—passes the piles of trash in the graveyard, the oil drum filled with wood and fire, passes, for all he knows, the skeleton his friend Toomey had seen, not rising from the ground, but laid in a corner, never buried, the bones as gray as the sky. Omar keeps his eyes on the tallest building on the street, where, on the fifth floor, he hopes to find his mother. A rent party.

He thinks about the baby on the train. Its eyes closed, wrapped in a green sweater, its mother's—sister's?—enfolding arms swaying with the rhythm of the railcar. More than wanting to live with his own mother, and long before even stepping on that train, before stepping on countless trains, Omar had wanted a baby boy of his own. But only you know that.

Winston, thirteen, takes the handkerchief from his pocket and wipes the spittle from his grandfather's chin. The old man turns the key in the ignition of the truck. It's older than Winston, abandoned in their back-yard for almost as long as the boy can remember. The boy had shoveled leaves and twigs—a bird's nest?—from the seats before they'd entered. The windshield is cracked in the corner—no hair or blood, simply a crack, a rock left on a road years before. Unlike his grandfather, who is gaunt, mostly bones, skeletal, Winston is a big boy, bigger than most in his school. Fat. Fat fingers, fat toes. He's only eleven but thinks as he gains age he might gain the person inside himself whom he wishes to be. The old man, his name is Winston too, coughs, and Winston wipes again with the handkerchief.

The truck is not going to turn over. The engine in the truck—the starter—is not going to turn over. Winston looks out the windshield and sees, in the distance, the sunflower fields bending with the wind. To the left he sees the lights—green and red—of the Ferris wheel of the trav-eling carnival. From this distance, a long distance away, it looks slow, but when he'd sat in one of the cars with his father, it had seemed fast, rising and falling above the lights of the spook house and the ticket mer-chants—and he hopes, if the starter turns over, that he and his grand-father might drive there. Might ride the Ferris wheel together. In his pocket he carries all the money he has to his name (seven dollars and change). But the starter won't turn. Winston, the grandson, knows little about trucks or cars, but thinks, as his grandfather turns the key, that something is being burned out. That the more the key turns, the more something is being lost.

He'd ridden the Ferris wheel only once. Had not budgeted—his father's word—correctly, and had left that seven dollars and change at home. He'd blown most of his money on the spook house, which his father had refused to ride with him. He'd sat alone, that first time, in the front car, had screamed when the dragon had bent at the entrance, fire glowing in its belly, and had assumed (Winston) that he'd be scorched before he even got inside the house. The pirates had swiped their sabers above his head, a witch boiled the skulls of children in her cauldron, and the bony white hands of skeletons had barely reached him, clicking against the top of the rail car. The giants appeared after that. I want it to be quiet in here, the man in the car behind him had said, and it was only then that Winston could hear his own screams, had felt for a moment outside himself, had wondered, hearing that man's voice, what his class-mates might think of him. I can't help it, he'd said, I'm scared. Had said that with the weight of the two dollars he'd paid for the ride. Two dollars, he felt, earned him the right to scream. More pirates had been next, and the goblins after that. Finally, the ghosts, white sheets, through which he could make out the people, and he did not feel so afraid. But he contin-ued to scream, wanting his two dollars' worth, until the cars exited the house and he saw his father waiting near the ticket booth, arms crossed, the Ferris wheel turning in the black sky behind him.

Looks like you were scared, said his father.

No, Winston had said. I loved it.

The starter turns over. Winston looks behind him, through the glass of the rear window of the truck. A thick cloud of smoke—as big as a giant's fist—blows out into the air. Beyond, Winston can see an orange glow, not the sun, which was setting in the opposite direction, but some-thing else, something almost as big, glowing and stretching toward the sky.

His grandfather says nothing, has said nothing for almost a week. He switches the gears into Drive, and the truck sets off across the yard, spit-ting a trail of white smoke and mud.

A boxer's defense is designed to prevent the jabs, hooks, and crosses of her opponent from reaching the vulnerable areas. It is also intended to leave her in a position from which she might score with her own punches. A boxer avoids an opponent's blows by using correct techniques in blocking, parrying, ducking, and slipping.

Helen showers, dresses, ices down her left elbow where a bruise has already formed. She waits for her trainer at the ringside of the gym, watches two young men wrap each other up near the ropes. An older man separates them, gives them a silent count, steps away, and the shorter of the two men takes a shot to the head, swings wildly, and is hit again. Helen examines her cut lip in the reflection of the windows. She waits for her trainer for a half hour, watches the two men in the ring. When she gives up, she exits through the back door, walks through a cloud of cigarette smoke, the stares of the boxers, walks the long road home in the dark.

She unlocks the house quietly. Her mother is likely asleep. In the kitchen, Helen takes her brother, two years old, from his daybed, wakes him, wipes his nose with the sleeve of her shirt. She sets him on his feet, steadying him with her hands gripped beneath his arms.

Her father was a pilot when she was younger, had a prop plane that he flew out of Juneau, ferrying supplies to homesteaders, taking Helen with him on occasion. She'd sit at the window as he flew low over the inside waterway, watching for pods of orcas or the hump of gray whales against the white crests of the sea. On the brightest days, the green treetops stretched for as far as she could see, and her father, holding his hand up against the sun, blinded from the horizon, seemed to fly on instinct. When they reached the lighthouse on Hawkins Point, they turned landward, flying over the black rocks and the white dots of eagles' heads, sharp and clear in the branches of the tallest evergreens. Even then, Helen knew life would not last this way, sensed that she would always come down, knew that high expectations led to disappointment.

When she'd left him—been sent away—she sat on the bollard of the ferryboat, alone in the stern, her face wrapped in scarves, watching her breath disappear in the mist from the ship's wake. The ferryboat pitched and rolled with the waves. Above the stern, a line of gulls stretched and dived at fish in the water.

Her baby brother neither smiles nor frowns, looks at her with great curiosity, moans for a moment, then is silent as she removes her hands, lets him stand on his own. The expression on his face changes, the first thought of doubt. His knees give way, and she catches him, leans forward and slips her hands against his ribs. On the ferryboat, she'd sat in the cabinhouse next to an old woman, had stored the woman's duffle bag in the rack above them where the woman could not reach, had stood on the armrest to pack it in. The woman had slipped her a piece of chocolate, and though Helen would have preferred to save it for later, to savor the thought of the candy waiting in her pocket, she ate it slowly, nibbling at the edges, letting the chocolate melt on her tongue. They'd played cards, she and the old woman, every afternoon on the three-day trip—gin rummy, crazy eights, and bird's cage—had eaten their soup on the starboard benches, had looked through the woman's binoculars at a sea otter, at the weekday fishermen pulling in their crab traps. She still wrote to Mrs. Lange, once each Christmas so far, and once in the summer, received letters back. Beneath the locks of gray hair, Helen had noticed the woman's ear, the top half missing, a stub on the skull, and the woman, noticing Helen's stare had said, A donkey bit that off. I got too close when I was a little girl. My father took that donkey out to the field and shot him after that.

Helen sets her brother straight again. Locks his knees into place. He continues to watch her, as if her hands, her arms, were connected to his own body. When she lets go, he watches the hands move away, his eyes begin to water. He takes a step toward her as she pulls away, keeps his feet. He wants those hands back. Takes another step, keeps his feet again, loses his balance, straightens himself, has a look of surprise for a moment, and in that moment loses his balance again. He falls back before she can snatch him up. He moves faster in that fall, it seems, than her trainer has ever moved, and before the child fully realizes he has fallen, she has him in her arms, pushes his head against her neck, begins a song that he recognizes. His fall is forgotten, if it ever happened at all.

What is it out there that points the right way? Omar feels this, although he doesn't think it, not exactly, as he makes his way through the snow-flakes mixed with rain, his feet slipping against the sidewalk. His thoughts are on his mother. When he opens the door to the tallest apart-ment building, the air is only slightly warmer, and a sourly unpleasant odor drifts from the hallway. He takes the steps one at a time, knows bet-ter than to trust the railing, passes a man at the top of the stairway who mutters, Works, man, works, takes the rest of the steps, moves faster, up to the fifth floor. He passes the people, the bottles in the hallway, finds the apartment and then the bedroom.

His mother is a small circle in the center of the bed. She is alone, and for that Omar is grateful. She is no longer the fat woman that his brother had spoken of, taking the belt through the broken window. She is skin and bones. He takes a cloth from his pocket, has brought it for this very purpose, runs cold water over it in the bathroom. Returns and wipes his mother's face. Touches the sores on her lips, wipes the blood away. She stirs, opens her eyes, closes them again. A dead rat lies in the corner of the room. You're good to come get me, she says, mumbles the words to the point that he can barely make them out, but he's heard them before. Soon she'll try to convince him this is as good a place to sleep as any, will ask him to slip up next to her. Let's go Mama, he says. In the ten minutes you want to sit here, we can be home.

She squeezes his hand, tries to sit up, leans back on her elbows. They can hear people begin to dance in the next room, can feel the bass of the stereo through the floorboards. Omar wishes he'd turned on the lights. He kisses her on the forehead, is trapped by her arms, still strong, even at this time. He looks out the window at the river. His mother, he is sure, is kind to other people, treats people better than anyone he knows. He believes his mother means everything to him. We could be at the bottom of the stairs in two minutes, he says to her.

Longer than that.

A year before, he used to look out on that river. He thought there might be another boy, a lot like him, on the other side, but now he doesn't think so. His mother rises, sits up, rubs his shoulders with her hand. Kisses him where he kissed her. She stands up from the bed and stumbles to the bathroom, and in seven minutes, they'll reach the bottom of the stairs.

That boy on the other side of the river, way on the other side, miles and states away, watches his father from the cab of the truck as his grandfather drives through the ruts and ridges of the back lawn. His father stands with arms limp at his sides, as surprised as the boy at the movement of the truck. The man disappears around the corner of the house—the two Winstons disappear around the corner of the house—and the truck creaks and bounces onto the state highway. Above them, the stars are clear. They drive on, slow; cars pass them on the left side as the older Winston shifts to higher, then lower gears. It seems to the younger Winston that his grandfather cannot decide on something. They drive in the direction of the carnival. Winston can see the Ferris wheel turn, remembers his father sitting next to him on the ride—the only ride the man took that day—and knows that the carnival is not his grandfather's destination.

Maybe the creek, he thinks, but not likely. If a raindrop fell in that creek it might travel south to a larger stream, and a river after that, might find its way to where three rivers meet, might choose the smallest of the three and turn eastward, rolling over rocks, fish, hollow reeds and old tires, rats. Might be observed from a rooftop by a boy near Winston's age. But Winston doesn't think of this. He thinks of the snake his grandfather had caught at the creek, had pinched it near the back of the head, lifted it from the mud, showed Winston how to hold it, watched as it crawled up the arm of his grandson, had seen the fear and the delight in the boy's face.

But they pass the turnoff for the creek, and soon after, they pass the carnival. Winston's eyes follow the Ferris wheel as it rises above them, a hundred yards from the shoulder of the road. The older Winston follows his grandson's gaze, watches the lights of the Ferris wheel in the rearview mirror. He has a clarity of thought for a change: that would've been a good place to stop. He has no idea where he is going, recognizes this fact, and in recognizing it, knows that he has come through the fog of his own thoughts which, God knows, he's been trying to come through for the past week.

But even as he keeps his eyes on the road, edges the steering wheel to the right, he keeps the picture of his grandson in his mind. The boy's father had considered him a halfwit. The word had bothered the older Winston. He'd seen it hang in the air like a weight, had thought he might keep it from settling around the boy's neck. On the days when the father worked, the old man had taught the boy how to drive the tractor in the fields of his neighbor's yard. The boy was tall for his age. His feet could touch the pedals if he sat forward. The old man thought he might teach the boy a trade. Farming took not great thoughts, but a focus that he was certain the boy had. He'd taught him how to bale hay and how to lead the cows in to milk, how to hook up the machines. He'd taught him how to catch a snake—that was for fun—and earlier still, years before, how to tie his shoes and how to read. He thought he might be teaching him something here, in the truck, had started the old clunker with that in mind, in his fogged mind, but what that was he was not now sure.

On the windshield the reflection of the carnival lights dim, and another set of lights shines brighter. Blue lights. The old man checks his mirror and sees the sheriff's cruiser closing the distance on the highway.

God dammit, he says.

Hey, says the younger Winston. That's your mouth.

The old man neither stops nor speeds up. The cruiser rides close to his bumper, and the lights glow strong against the windshield. The deputy switches on his siren, follows close, and when, after a minute— two minutes—have passed, calls in to the switchboard for backup. On a straightaway, he moves the cruiser to the left lane, comes even with the truck. Beyond them, down the highway, Winston can see the same glow he'd seen from the farmhouse. Not the carnival, and not even now the lights of the sheriff's cruiser, but a glow greater than any of those things, as bright as the moon, even at this distance. It burns orange against the skyline.

The deputy, now ten minutes past his shift, had taken the call because it was an easy one: an old man and a boy in a truck, to be pulled over and returned to a farmhouse five miles back. The deputy has a boy of his own, is a first-time father, had seen his boy walk two days before, had caught him as he fell, had been thinking about that as he called in for backup. He pulls level with the truck, in the opposite lane. They're not moving very fast. He smiles at the old man. Doesn't see any reason to be rude, had not been raised that way. He points to the side of the road.

The old man looks at this deputy. The man looks like a boy himself. The older Winston takes in the smile. Takes it for a cockiness that the deputy had not intended. The old man raises his right hand and extends his middle finger. Next to him, his grandson—a bit of a prude when it comes to language—likes that. The old man can hear the boy's laugh.

You do it, he says.

No way, says Winston.

The deputy loses the smile and sets his foot against the brake. Ahead, he can see a long line of cars, blocking the road in both directions, stretching toward an orange glow in the distance, bright as the moon. He seems to register this—the deputy does—thinks he might see the source of the glow and hopes he will not. Thinks of his son again, and then of the boy in the truck. He presses down on his brake and gives the old man some room.

Slipping is avoiding a blow by moving to the side, a counterpunch follows to the right if she moves to the right. A left from the left. A duck is a bend to escape an opponent's blow. The hands are held in punching position so she might retaliate as soon as the opponent's arm passes over her head.

Helen tapes her hands, makes fists as she sits on the sink in the kitchen, watches the shadow of her hands against the floor. Outside, she ties the punching bag to the largest low branch of the spruce pine, fifty yards from her house. She warms up, counts to four hundred on the bag, her fists working from memory. She watches her white breath in the air. She hits the bag like it was made of glass, hits it solid and light, hits it on the backswing so as not to break it. Years from now, will she stand on a corner at two in the morning, waiting for someone who never shows up? She thinks this at around three hundred. Wonders who that person might be. She sees the portholes and hatches of the ferryboat, feels the warmth of the bourbon slide down her throat, just a nip—Mrs. Lange's word—try it if you like it. She hadn't liked it at the time, but likes it now, doesn't taste the bitterness or the sting while punching at the bag. It warms her: the memory, the taste, and the movement around the tree.

Helen reaches four hundred, stops and moves to the other side of the bag, moves beyond glass, thinks of the bag as rubber, bouncing back, bouncing faster the harder she hits it, if she keeps the right rhythm. She thinks of her trainer. Then, tries to think of the ferryboat instead of him. He's twice and a half her age. He's ugly. She'd like to break his nose. Thinks that she might slip in one day, with practice, with repetition, with guile and deceit, and smack him a good one. She smacks the bag a good one and loses the rhythm, tries to get it back, fails. She stops the bag and starts again. The uppercut is a blow delivered with either hand and in close quarters. The boxer finds this blow most effective against an opponent boxing in a crouching position.

Omar crouches like a boxer, as if he's waiting for the blow to come, waiting for his chance to cross or jab, but he crouches for neither of those reasons. He holds the weight of his mother, half her weight. Even with her skin and bones, she is still heavier than him. He's a small boy. A squeak next to Winston, if they'd ever stand together, he's not as solid or defined as Helen. He holds his mother's weight up in the rain and sleet with his legs pressed with each step against the sidewalk. He accounts for a slip with each step, although he never falters, not any time between the apartment buildings, eight blocks. He keeps her talking, keeps her awake, lets her take her weight back, takes it on again.

I rode that bike down that hill, you remember, she says.

Omar doesn't know what she's talking about.

My mother said we'd go biking, and I used to fly. There was a group of boys, and when they saw me come by, one of them said, "That girl is too fast, we're going to have to cut her down." And I was like, that's right, cause I'm like a fast speed.

Okay, says Omar. I hear you. He wipes the rain from his eyes. They didn't catch you, did they?

Oh, they caught me.

C'mon Mama.

All right, she says. They're still chasing me. We better hurry up.

Omar looks ahead in the sleet and rain. They've got a long way to go yet. He takes on the weight. I won't let them get you tonight, he says.

They're off the road—Winston and his grandfather—they broke a fence and carved up a farmer's barren cornfield with the bald tires of the truck. If it had been before harvest, the older Winston would have stopped the truck. He's thinking smart now, wants to keep in motion. The sheriff's cruiser follows behind them, through the field; a scarecrow is run down, falls in the glow of the blue lights. The deputy switches on his wipers to get the straw off his windshield. Winston—the older one—sees the scarecrow fall in his rearview mirror, thinks about how someone had stuffed the old shirt and pants, painted the face, maybe a mother and her kids. He doesn't think much of the deputy for knocking it over. He—Winston—is senile and dying, and even he'd thought to turn the wheel.

The younger Winston thinks this is great fun. Better than the spook ride and the Ferris wheel put together and then some. Yet he knows, can feel in his bones, that they'd paid no admission price, that they'll pay a price at the end of this ride instead. He wants this ride to go on and on, so that they won't have to pay. He feels that his grandfather will pay a large price, and yet he senses that he—the younger Winston—himself will pay longer. Will not lose his seven and a half dollars, but will lose something else when the ride ends. It's like driving the tractor—don't tell your father, the old man had said—and he feels this same dread, this same delight, as they come clear of the fields. Winston looks back now through the window at the blue lights of the sheriff's cruiser, and farther still, the orange glow a mile down the road.

And then they're in the sunflower field. The old man chooses not to avoid it, can't see a way around it. Tall stalks fall in the lights of the truck, the blue lights of the sheriff's cruiser flashing against the windshield, the yellow heads of flowers snapping and falling against the hood of the truck, flying through the side windows. The younger Winston collects the heads of the yellow flowers in his lap, listens to the pops and snaps of the stalks against the fenders, the tires. The flowers reach in the window like arms, like the hands of skeletons. When they come clear of the field, the silence seems to swallow him.

Ahead, right in front of them, he sees the ditch; they both do, but too late. Their brake lights warn the deputy, who slows in time to avoid it, but the front end of the truck, its wheels spinning in air, smashes into the opposite bank. Winston feels himself falling, feels the thick fingers of his grandfather's hand against his chest, but it was the seatbelt that saved him, saved his grandfather too. He hears now, seconds later when it seems quiet, after the deputy has switched off his siren, the shatter of the windshield. He sees the broken blue shards on his lap, on his shoes near the floorboard. The yellow heads of sunflowers lie on the floor. The boy believes he's bleeding to death. He studies his arms, his ankles.

You cut? says his grandfather.

I don't think so.

His grandfather has a gash on his hand, a small one. There's a little blood there.

You ready to run? says his grandfather.

Winston is still looking for a death wound. Let's stay here, he says.

The old man looks through the back window. I got to keep moving, he says. Already, they can see the white beam of the deputy's flashlight through the back window.

Come or go, says the old man. He opens his door and kicks off the glass. He moves faster than Winston has ever seen him move.

Let's stay here, says Winston. He doesn't want to touch the glass in his lap.

I'll see you again, says the old man. And he's off, out of the truck. Winston can hear him splash in the creek. The boy thinks of snakes. He watches as the old man's white head disappears from the flashing blue light. It enters the darkness beyond Winston's sight.

The deputy watches the old man go. He calls out for him to stop. He thinks about his training, moves beyond it for a moment. He could plug the old man in the leg: he's a good shot. It's not much of a distance. But, he doesn't even unlatch his holster. He climbs down into the creek, feels the water soak his boots and socks, slips a little in the mud.

You all right? he says to the boy. He shines the flashlight in the boy's face, checks for firearms, a knife to the heart. The boy is terrified.

That your grandfather?

The boy nods.

He got a gun on him? Any weapons?

The boy shakes his head. He won't hurt nobody.

He almost killed you, says the deputy.

Winston doesn't like the man's tone. It reminds him of his teachers at school, the way they mix concern with a shake of their heads, the downward turn of their lips. You can do better. This is all right, good even, but you need to concentrate, focus, you know what I mean?

I don't, says Winston.

You don't what? says the deputy.

I don't know.

All right, says the man. He unclips the latch on his holster. You stay here. I'll be back in a few minutes.

Winston watches the man's head—black hair—disappear out of the blue lights. The boy picks off the glass with his fingertips, drops the shards on the floorboard. Nicks his finger with the last one, puts the finger in his mouth, tastes the blood. He is sure he has betrayed his grandfather. Doesn't exactly know how, but is sure. He picks the yellow flowers off after that. When he climbs out of the cab, splashes into the water, crawls up the bank of the ditch on hands and knees, muddying both, he is convinced that the accident, the ride even, is his fault. He watches the blue lights hover across and around the ditch, and he watches for the white and black heads in the creek. Can see neither. A woman in the farmhouse has come out onto the porch. She stands at the railing, arms crossed, looking at her sunflower field, looks at where Winston is looking.

He sucks at his finger, tastes no blood, wishes he had left with his grandfather. He feels completely alone at the edge of the ditch. Abandoned maybe. Feels like no one—not his grandfather, not the deputy, not his father, not the woman on the porch—will ever return to him. Behind him, he hears the hum of the engine, not from the truck, but from the deputy's cruiser. When he turns, he sees, in the flash of the blue lights, the keys hanging in the ignition switch.

The left hook is a short, bent-arm blow, thrown off the left foot, as the boxer turns her body to the right behind the punch. The right cross, a short or long blow, is thrown off the trailing right foot and crosses the opponent's right arm. The body is turned to the left, with the left arm and hand in the guard position.

Helen opens the window on the second floor, pops out the screen. She takes her baby brother out onto the rooftop. She likes it up here, believes her brother does too. She looks down at him. He's wrapped in a sweater and blanket. She rocks him against her shoulder.

She remembers the coastline from the ferryboat. The waves of the sea breaking against the black rocks, seeming to continue toward the mountains. The mountains seemed as waves themselves, the landscape of the sea the same as land. She'd thought this, had said it to Mrs. Lange, and Mrs. Lange, holding her cards to the tip of her chin, had stared out at the sea, at the Inside Passage. In that moment, a man with a cast on his arm had crossed the deck. It does look like that, the old woman had said. They seem to go on and on.

Helen remembers this. She hums a tune to her brother, rocks him in rhythm with her thoughts. Sleeping beside Mrs. Lange that night, she'd heard the woman mumble in her sleep. She was sure she'd not misheard. You're not going to let another man hit you like that. They were alone, no man around. Helen had sipped at the flask of bourbon, her second taste, still bitter and harsh in her throat. She looked down at her cards. Solitaire. Felt the dip and roll of the ship for the first time that day. Heard someone latch a porthole closed. She'd played a card.

Now, she feels the warmth of the child against her shoulder, feels herself slip on the roof. She presses her feet against the shingles, holds her brother tight against her shoulder. Tomorrow, the trainer: she's going to break his nose.

Winston finds it—the sheriff's cruiser—a lot easier to drive than the tractor. His feet meet the pedals easily. He turns off the radio, grips his hands on the wheel, keeps the tires away from the edge of the ditch. He's moving faster than the tractor, than on any ride at the carnival. After only a minute—two—he can see the nods and dips of the two heads in the stream, the one behind closing the distance.

Behind him, the older Winston can hear the footfalls, the splashes of the deputy. In his youth, he'd have left the man far behind. Twenty years ago he would have left him behind, had always been a good runner. The ditch reminds him of France, near the Moselle River, of a ditch he'd run through in the war. Artillery in the distance, and German voices behind him. He kept low and kept the pace. He outran them. And later he was shot in the back by another American, a boy—he'd always assumed—who shot at everything. He lay that night in a foxhole. His wound was packed but not sewn. The pain was distant, a dull morphine pleasure. The foxhole was deep and he'd stayed quiet. He was nineteen and watched the snow and the tracers falling from the sky.

Blue lights above him now in the ditch. He glances behind him. The deputy is closing the distance. The old man hears his grandson's voice, and up the ditch he goes. He is not without skills, even with his mind failing. He gets into the cruiser. Shuts the door. He puts his seat belt on. He wants to be a good example for the boy.

The younger Winston takes out the handkerchief; there's spittle hanging off the old man's chin and he wipes it away. Carefully. He wants to apologize, for not following, but he can't quite make the words. It's a ride, he thinks. This whole thing. He wants it to go on and on. Through the windshield he can see the orange glow in the distance. It's just over the next hill. They can make the road easy from here. The boy can feel— even as he presses on the pedal, even as the cruiser moves forward, even as he tries to say what he has to say again—the hand of the deputy on his arm, through the window, a vice, like one of his teacher's at school. The boy presses hard on the pedal, lets go the handkerchief.

The deputy, his other hand on the rooftop, hesitates, feels the slap of mud against his legs, feels the motion of the cruiser, feels his boots dragged across rocks. He can imagine his head run over in blue lights. He thinks about his baby son, decides, lets go of the boy's arm. As he slides to the ground, the back tire rolls over the man's boot, breaking five bones and fracturing two more.

When they reach the apartment, Omar sets his mother against the wall, closes the door behind them, pulls her up before she can sit down, presses his hands against her ribs. He looks up the stairway. Two minutes you think? he says.

Three.

Three then. He wipes the snow and rain from her hair, off the crown of her nose and cheeks. He wraps her arm around his shoulder and takes the stairs, letting her lead, pushes at the small of her back.

Why you pushing? she says.

I'm trying to help.

You're being rude.

I'm not meaning.

Meaning and doing are two different things. Your brother never pushed his mother like you do.

Omar says nothing.

If your brother was here, I'd already be up these stairs.

He takes his hand from her back.

Don't make that face, she says.

I'm not.

I'm looking at your face and you're making it right now.

He hides that face, looks down at the stairway, sees the cracks in the wood, a dark stain on the floorboards. He waits, listens to the silence between them. In that silence, she takes his hand, squeezes it, leads him up the stairs. As he follows her, he feels as if he's learning a trick. He's adding to his bag of tricks: keep her talking, wipe her face with cold water, give her a goal—five minutes, three, ten. Turn on the lights. Pout a little. He's going to get this right.

She stops on the staircase with a flight and a half to go. Give me a push, she says. These old bones aren't going to make it.

It's a wood yard, says the younger Winston. They sit at a roadblock, the blue lights still flashing above them. Another deputy walks down the line of cars ahead of them. He's checking licenses, looking in backseats. Behind him, dark smoke pushes across the road. The fire in the wood yard is a deep orange, tinges of blue and white in the center. It's a huge fire—even many miles back, a deputy with a broken foot can see it. But it puts the younger Winston in mind of the carnival. He remembers the spook house and the fire in the dragon's belly. He'd screamed, though he doesn't scream now. He's tempted though. He watches the firemen spraying white mists of water over the blaze. They'll not put it out for a long while. By the time the road is open again: another boy, miles and states away from here, will have unlaced his mother's shoes, tipped a mug of water to her lips, pulled the curtains closed from the glow of the moonlight. He'll take a blanket from his own bed, Omar, cover his mother. He'll slip in next to her and sleep. But Winston doesn't think of this. He can't see any of these things. He sees the fire only. Even at this distance, he can feel the heat of the blaze.

The older Winston has a fog in his mind. He's confused, but at least he knows it. But he doesn't know if the fog is coming in or going out. He sees, ahead of them, another deputy. The one checking the licenses. Three cars ahead. The man wears a cowboy hat. Silhouetted against the fire the deputy looks like a bandit, or the Lone Ranger. The deputy gives the license back, sees the blue lights. He looks. He knows this cruiser, but he doesn't know the two people in it. He passes the next car. Keeps his eyes on the two Winstons. But he doesn't know their names. He holds his hand up to shield against the lights. He tries to see into the cruiser, he's level with the car ahead. He studies these two people in the cruiser. The older Winston feels the fog slipping in.

The younger Winston, he's been waiting. He has his hand on the seat between them. What do you want to do? he says. He's said it three times now. There's no answer. He grips the edge of the seat hard. Looks at the deputy.

He wants then to reach into his pocket. Take out his wallet. Pay the deputy. But the man doesn't approach the car. Winston wants to pay the price for this ride now, before the price is named. He thinks the ride might could go on. Thinks maybe if he moves fast enough, he might get a bargain. He believes the price to be paid will not be found in his pocket. He reaches there anyway. The deputy, watching the boy, doesn't see a boy. It's a big boy. It's an adult. The boy's hand reaches for something, and the deputy unclips his holster.

The older Winston reaches forward. He's not sure if he's got this right, but he reaches out of sight of the deputy. The younger Winston watches the hand go. He wants that hand to go on and on, knows that the ride is still on, as long as that hand moves, as long as the deputy's hand moves, the ride will not end. The old man flips his wrist and the engine dies. His hands are still moving. He takes up his grandson's hands, slowly. He's gentle, this man, with this boy. Always. He puts their hands on the steering wheel.

The uppercut is a blow delivered—well—up, with either hand and in close quarters. The boxer finds this blow most effective against an opponent boxing in a crouched position and moving in.

It's the morning. Helen walks the three miles to the gym in a white fog that hovers over the gravel and the farmland in wisps and strings, in fingers. She smells smoke and watches the first orange rays sift through the white fog.

She's been told where the key is. She undresses near the ring, hears the door open across the way. Slips into her shorts and T-shirt. She tapes her hands, and watches her trainer undress, tape his hands. She skips rope. Three hundred.

In the ring they say nothing. She ties his left glove. They crouch in the center of the ring. He ties her left, then her right, shows her again how to tie with a glove on. How to make do. They take a minute in their corners. Here, they are their own trainers. When she talks to herself, she sees his face. She listens to his instructions.

In his corner, he sees a girl. Not this girl—the one behind him—but another girl. He sees his mother as a child. He's seen her in black-and-white photographs, and he remembers a story now. His mother is nine years old and reaches for a piece of fruit in a street cart. He can't remember the fruit now. Let's call it an orange. His mother is looking like a buyer, but she means to steal that orange. Her brother lies in a bed, asleep. When the boy—the boxer's uncle—wakes, someone will wipe his chin, will help him walk, might offer a piece of fruit. The boy will not live out the year. But his sister reaches for an orange in a cart on the street with a picture of her brother in her mind. She has black curls and tiny hands. She watches the merchant, pretends to be a buyer. She squeezes the orange while her brother, blocks and blocks away, sleeps, while the merchant turns, while, years and decades later, Helen says, Ready?

The trainer turns and looks at this other girl.

Do you know what I'm going to do? he says.

No.

This merchant. Decades before. Let's give him a moustache. He sees the girl. The merchant is quick and tall, and two steps away. He's got long arms and angry hands, and he's caught his share of thieves in his day. This little girl looks at him. She's nine years old, but will one day be someone's mother. She puts the orange into her pocket. Brazen. Her

eyes ask him a question: are you as fast as I am? He doesn't have to answer the question. He believes he's plenty fast. He moves, sudden, and
grabs her. He's going to show her now. He's going to show what he does
to thieves.

But he is completely mistaken. He looks at his hands. He holds nothing. And now he has one less orange. He grabbed air. He looks around
for the girl, for the boxer's mother. But she's long gone. She's slipped
away. Because that is what a fast speed does.

The trainer moves away from his corner.

Do you know what you're going to do? he says.

Yes, says Helen.

What's that?

Keep moving, she thinks, but she says nothing. She lets go of the
ropes, fits her mouthpiece to her teeth, walks to the center of the ring,
meets him, and moves in.

THE BOOTS

It was a visiting priest, as it often was, and the two altar boys half-listened to the homily and stared out at the small congregation. Snow was falling fast outside, and many of the old people had stayed home, but there was one man—more ancient than any they'd seen—sitting in the back of the church, and he was obviously a homeless man and a little drunk tonight. At least it seemed this way to Omar, the older of the two altar boys, and he watched the man close his eyes and lean forward, almost asleep, then catch himself and listen again to the homily. The priest had moved past grace and love, as if they might be near the bottom of a list, but important to mention nonetheless. When he spoke the words "Lazarus" and "resurrection" the two boys perked up, because that story was often interesting to them. "When his name was called he awakened," the priest said. "Just as our names are called, every day. And we must awake in a similar way." And then the priest went on to some parish announcements. It made Omar frown. He'd been hoping for some new information. He looked over at Lewis, but Lewis did not return the look. The younger boy's head jerked to the side, and then again, as if beyond the priest's homily he could also hear some music that no one else could hear. It was a bad tic and had become worse in the last year. He'd been told he might eventually—when he was older—shake to death, and he'd shared this secret with Omar, who had told him not to worry over it too much, and who'd said, no, he wouldn't tell anyone else.

They went through the rest of mass, ringing the bells when it was called for and taking the gifts back to the altar, and during communion they held the little dishes under the chins of the parishioners, though no one had dropped a host in a long while. It had been a year, and Omar had caught it, and the priest—another visitor, though not this one—had told him that he was a very vigilant young man, and this had delighted both boys, so much so that they'd gone to the dictionary and looked up the word: "watchful and awake, alert to avoid danger." They liked that. When mass was over, they walked down the aisle and waited at the back of the church with the priest as he shook hands with some of the parishioners, and some of the people shook the hands of Omar and Lewis, or patted them on the head, and when this happened the boys smiled though they weren't smiling on the inside. They watched the poor box as some people dropped in dollars and coins, and even the ancient man dropped something in, and when everyone had left the boys took up the box and brought it back to the sacristy and opened it and counted out the money.

It was not much: four dollars and change, plus a candy wrapper, a book of matches, and a little white bone that they picked up and studied. It was just a few inches long and seemed like it might be half the wishbone of a turkey or a chicken, and they wondered about the wish that had been made upon it. Good health maybe, or a change in the weather. They placed it at the top of the stack of money and took it away to the priest, who was preparing himself for confessional.

Once—the year before Omar arrived—there had been a five-dollar bill in the poor box, and Lewis had slipped this into his pocket. He'd bought nine cans of lemon soda with the money and drank them all in one day. He felt bad about it now. He'd felt bad about it for a long time, and he'd been sneaking a quarter into the pile for the last few months. In a few more weeks he'd have it all paid back.

They offered the money to the priest, and the man took it and put it in a drawer, and Lewis stood there with the bone in his open hand. The priest looked at it.

"What the hell is that?" he said.

"It was in the box," said Lewis, and his head jerked to the side.

"Somebody offered it up," said Omar.

"Well, get rid of it," said the priest.

The two boys studied the bone.

"Can we keep it?" said Lewis.

The priest frowned. His expression seemed to indicate that the bone was a great inconvenience to him.

"I don't care," he said, and though there were altar dressings to fold and the chalice and the dishes to wash, and the wine to be poured back into the bottle, the two boys followed the priest out to the confessional where there were two women waiting in the pews just outside. Later, the two boys would try to guess the sins to be confessed: adultery and jealousy and murder and thievery and sloth, the latter of which was the worst as far as Omar was concerned, but now they waited for the priest to open the door to the confessional, and when he saw them standing behind him he said, "What do you want?"

"Can we see in?" said Omar.

The priest looked at his side of the confessional. "In here?" he said.

"Yes."

He seemed to consider that, and he looked over at the two women who were praying with their eyes closed.

"Does Father Ramon let you see in?"

They frowned at that and said that he didn't.

The priest sighed, opened the door, and waved them in, and immediately they asked if they could slide the windows open, and he said to keep their voices down and yes that was all right if they were quick about it.

So, they opened and closed the windows and they each had a seat in the chair. The other leaned outside to see if the little light came on, and when it did he gave the thumbs-up. They asked the priest if one of them could go around and kneel on the other side of the confessional, and the priest said no, go on now, and so they did, back up to the altar and the sacristy where they washed and folded and put things away, and when they were done they put on their coats and scarves and headed out into the snow.

There was a strong and painful windstorm outside, and the two boys headed straight into it, wiping the snow from their eyes and moving from streetlight to streetlight in the dark. The lid of a trashcan blew across the road, and the cars parked near the sidewalk were covered in white, like a long line of sand dunes or mountains in a range. The boys crunched along in the drifts, and Omar thought of his mother, as he often did. He'd not been vigilant enough with her—she'd been a heavy drinker and had died of it—but he tried to put that from his mind, and instead he remembered waiting for her at the laundry in the hospital, watching her sort and weigh the linens that she pulled from baskets and oversized sacks. The room was long and filled with light, and he could hear nothing above the din of the washers and the fifty-gallon tanks filled with bleach water. His mother worked slow and deliberate in her long bib overalls, and every so often she'd motion for him to fold this stack of towels, these pillowcases, and they'd play an unnamed game: a poke to her ribs when she wasn't looking, and a pinch on his ear when he wasn't. Omar kept a tally in his head. He was always way ahead. They took up the sheets together and placed them in the washers.

When the boys arrived at the diner, just past the butcher's shop, they went in and found a booth in the corner. There was some music playing from the jukebox, something slow and bouncy, and the two boys bobbed their heads to the music as they studied the menus. They looked at the pictures of the french toast and the patty melt and the banana pie. There was a line of syrup caked at the top of Lewis' menu, and he scraped it off with the edge of his fingernail. They counted out their money, and figured in for a tip, and while they waited on the waitress they looked out at the snow that was swirling down into the streetlights. Omar imagined the moon and the stars falling to earth.

"What's it going to be?" said the waitress.

"A tea, please," said Omar.

"With two spoons, please," said Lewis.

She looked at them. "That's all you're going to order, isn't it?"

They said that it was, and sorry about that, and she took up their menus and went off into the kitchen.

Lewis took out the bone and placed it on the table halfway between them. His head jerked to the side. It was a strange little bone, they both agreed, and they began to play the football game with it. They slid the

bone across the table to each other, trying to score a touchdown by getting the bone to hang off the edge without falling. They tapped it with
the ends of their fingers. It was not easy, and they worked at it for a
while, and at some point Lewis observed that the table had not been
wiped down in a long time. Still, he was the first to score, a lucky shot
that ricocheted off the sugar container. Lewis lined the bone up for the
extra point, and when he flicked it, it went over Omar's shoulder and
into the soup of the man sitting behind them.

"What the hell?" the man said.

They turned to look at him, and the man was dressed in a red Santa
Claus suit. He looked very drunk and not very happy about the bone.

"Sorry," said Omar.

"This is a finger bone," said the man.

"Sorry," said Lewis.

"You threw a finger bone in my soup," said the man.

Their tea came then, with two spoons and two little containers of
cream.

"What are you yelling at these boys about?" said the waitress.

"Look," said the man. He pointed at his soup. "Finger bone."

The two boys went back out into the wind and the snow. They were filled
up with a cup of tea and two refills, and Omar had the bone in his pocket.
The man had not given it up easily, and they weren't allowed to play the
football game anymore. The snow was coming down sideways now, and
they walked into it, back toward the church. Lewis' tic was worse, harder
than before and more frequent, so that he began to have trouble walking
in a straight line. He took hold of the tail of Omar's coat and followed
the boy into the wind.

When they came to the church they could see that there was a strange
form under the light by the side door, and they trudged up toward it until
they could see that it was a man lying facedown on the steps. The man
was bundled in a heavy coat and scarf, and he had no shoes on his stocking feet. The boys circled around him and stopped near the hat lying

alone and covered with snowflakes. Lewis brushed it off and gave it a quick snap against his knee, and he placed it back on the man's head.

They turned the man over and they could see that it was the priest, the visiting one, and he was alive though he seemed fast asleep, and his face was cold to the touch. They found his wallet and the keys to the church in his pocket, and they dragged him inside to the sacristy and closed the door from the cold and the wind.

A cushion was found for his head, and a blanket to put over him. Omar ran warm water over a cloth and wiped the man's face. After a time, the priest opened his eyes and looked up at the boys. He seemed as if he was still half-asleep.

"What happened?" he said.

"Somebody rolled you," said Omar.

"They took your boots," said Lewis.

The man looked down at his socks. "Did they get the wallet?"

Omar held it in his hand, and he opened it so that the priest could see inside. There were many dollars in the wallet.

"Do you want a doctor?" said Omar.

"No. I want you to bring me some wine."

The boys looked to the cabinet where the wine was kept. The key was hanging there in the lock.

"You should go get your boots," said Omar. "I can show you where."

The priest looked up at the two boys. He squinted in the lights. "Leave me alone," he said, and he set his head back on the cushion and closed his eyes.

The boys walked for many miles. When they came to the bridge Omar took Lewis' hand, not for warmth, but because the younger boy was afraid of the water below. They walked carefully over the ice and crossed to the other side.

They found the address they'd been told about—an old foundry building, now falling apart—and they went inside, through a gash in the wall, and they walked past the broken glass and the blocks of old granite and concrete. Behind one of the piles of rocks they found the spiraled staircase. There were little white Christmas lights strung all down the banister, and the boys followed them down. Down and down. The little lights twisted below them like a long, beautiful water snake down into the dark. Both boys had the bad shivers, and they held their collars tight about their necks. Lewis remembered the face of the priest, and his head jerked to the side. It put him in mind of the bodies he'd seen at funerals. The expressions on the faces of the dead: lonely, it seemed to him, and sometimes deep in thought, as if the dead person was about to say something but didn't. He'd asked Father Ramon once could he touch the hand or maybe the feet of a dead man, a parishioner they'd known, and for that Lewis had been sent out to clean the statue of Saint Joseph with soap and water and an old toothbrush. He'd done the work gently, and with some care, because he was Lewis' favorite: not the priest, but Saint Joseph.

When they reached the end of the staircase they came to an open doorway, and the room on the other side seemed warm to them. They looked inside, and there was a large fireplace that was lit with coals. The coals burned orange and blue, and they shed a warm light on the rest of the room. There were candles on the walls and a small desk in the center of the room. A very large man, old and with long, stringy white hair, sat at the desk and was writing quickly in a thick tablet. All around the man were wooden shelves, tall and wide, and they were arranged in some kind of maze, and when the boys entered it they could see, in the firelight, what the shelves held.

Boots and shoes and more boots, of all sizes and makes and all manner of repair that they could imagine. Some were in pairs and some were alone, not set carefully but dropped, it seemed, in some random pattern, some laces tied together and some not. There were men's shoes and women's and many small shoes, so that some of them must have belonged to toddlers or even babies at one time. There were hundreds of them, and as the boys studied the shelves, the large gray man looked up from his ledger and said, "Hey!"

"Hey," said the boys, and they moved closer to the shelves. There was a pair of white sneakers near them, each with a little hole in the tip, as if the big toes had worn them through.

"How did you get in here?" said the man.

"We walked down the stairs," said Omar.

"I liked the lights," added Lewis.

The man frowned at that. He set his pen aside. "Who told you about this place?"

"A child," said Omar.

"And how did he know about it?"

"She," said Omar.

The man's expression didn't change. He looked at them impatiently. "She, then. How did she know about this place?"

"Our friends know a lot of things," said Omar.

The man leaned forward, as if he was trying to bring the two boys into focus.

"Come here," he said.

They walked up to the desk and looked at the man. He was old, though they could not guess the age, and his eyes seemed very tired. He had his hands placed over the writing tablet, and there were other sheets of paper with long lists of names set next to the tablet. A thin film of coal dust covered many of the items on the desk. A lantern was set at the edge of the desk and there were shelves behind the man and two wooden chairs leaning against the shelves.

"What do you want?" the man said.

"The boots," said Omar.

"Whose boots?"

"The priest's," said Lewis, and his head jerked to the side.

"What's wrong with your head?" the man said.

Lewis looked at the floor. "There's nothing wrong with my head."

The man studied them for a moment. He turned the lantern up so that he could see them better.

"What's this priest's name?"

The boys looked at each other. They didn't know the man's name. He hadn't been all that friendly. Omar thought about taking a guess.

"What's your name?" he said instead.

"I can't tell you that," said the man.

"Why not?"

"It's not allowed."

They stood there and studied the man, then the desk. They looked about at the shoes. The boys had stopped their shivers, and the glow from the fireplace was warm. They reached an agreement without saying anything, and they pulled up the two chairs and sat down in front of the desk.

"Hey, now," said the man. "I have work to do."

"What kind of work?" said Lewis.

The man pointed to the tablet. "I have to get all of these names written down tonight."

He still held one hand over the tablet, and the boys looked there. They waited. The man reached over and turned the lantern back down so they couldn't see what he'd written.

"You can't look here," said the man.

"Why not?" said Omar.

"Because it's not allowed."

"There's a lot of things not allowed here," said Lewis.

"That's right," said the man. "There are. And one thing that is not allowed is visitors. So if that's all, I expect you'll be going now."

"Okay," said Omar. "We just need the boots."

The man pointed at the boy. "You're not getting any boots," he said, and when he lifted his hand to point, the boys looked at the names on the tablet. They read as fast as they could, upside down. The man quickly slammed the book shut. It was an old book, and dust blew up across the desk.

"Now you've done it," the man said, and he wiped his fists into his eyes. "There's so much dust here. It comes from the coal." He looked at them. His eyes were filled with tears. "This is your fault."

Lewis got up from his chair. He reached into his pocket and handed his handkerchief to the man.

The man frowned, looked at the boy. Then he took the handkerchief and wiped his eyes. The dust was floating about the lantern, like little bugs in the yellow light.

"Not many people carry a handkerchief anymore," said the man.

"They ought to," said Lewis.

The man nodded. "Yes, they should." He wiped his eyes again, then unfolded the cloth. He held it up in the light. "This is a very nice hand-kerchief."

"I'll trade you it for the boots," said Lewis.

"No," said the man. "Thank you, though. Why are you concerned about these boots? They're not your boots. How well do you know this priest?"

"Not very well," said Omar.

"Then why do you care?"

The boys thought about that for a while. They looked down at their own shoes, and the man, after a time, looked down at them as well. He studied Omar's quickly, then Lewis'. He studied Lewis' shoes for a long time. A strange expression came over his face, something sad and dis-tant. He sat back in the chair and began to fold the handkerchief.

"We take our responsibilities very seriously," said Omar.

The man smiled at that. He set the cloth aside. "I'm sure you do. That's to be commended. That's also something that's gone out of style. Can I ask you your names?"

They told him, and he picked up his pen. He looked at the ledger. He paused, and then he set his pen back down. "Those are very nice names. I deal often with names, and those are most excellent. I like those very much. I'm sorry, I'm going to have to ask you to leave now. It's been very nice visiting with you. I don't get many visitors here, and you two have been among the finest. Do you think you can find your way out?"

"We'll just follow the lights," said Lewis.

"That's right, just follow the lights."

"They're really nice."

"Do you think so?" said the man. "That was a touch I put on the place. I wasn't sure that anyone would notice. Thank you for saying that. It's been awfully nice to meet you. Lewis. And Omar. I guess this is good-bye, then."

"Goodbye," said Omar.

"Goodbye," said Lewis.

The man picked up his pen. "Goodbye, then."

"There's the matter of the boots, though," said Omar.

"Yes," said Lewis. "We'll still have to settle that."

The man opened the book and began copying names. "I think it's good and settled," he said. "I think that has been well discussed. I'm sorry if you're not satisfied on that matter."

"No," said Omar. "We're not satisfied at all."

"Not even close," said Lewis, and he pointed accusingly toward the man's desk. "I think you were going to steal my handkerchief."

The man looked up. He was quite indignant. "I certainly was not."

Omar shook his head. "If you wanted it you could just have asked for it. I'm sure Lewis would have given it to you."

"I would have," said Lewis. He put his hands on his hips. "If he'd only asked."

"I don't want your stupid handkerchief," said the man. He picked it up and held it out for the boy.

"No," said Lewis. His head jerked to the side. "If you want it that bad you can have it."

"I don't want it at all," said the man. The handkerchief was still there, held out for Lewis.

Omar reached into his pocket then. He took out the bone and placed it on the desk. He slid it forward for the man.

"What's that?" said the man. He pulled back the handkerchief.

"It's a bone," said Omar.

"Finger bone," said Lewis.

The man looked at it. "That's disgusting," he said.

"It's all we have," said Omar.

"Well it's not enough," said the man.

"For what?" said Lewis.

"For the boots."

"So you will trade for them?" said Omar.

The man crossed his arms over his chest. He was looking very cross, and it put the boys in mind of Father Ramon when they asked to see the confessional. "Look, now," the man said. "There's not going to be any trade. I've got work to do here. The boots come in, all right? They come in and I write the names down in this book, and then that's it. All right?"

Lewis' head jerked to the side. "You write the names down?"

"Yes."

"And then that's it?"

"Yes, then that's the end, I'm afraid. I'm sorry. It's not pleasant work, but that's it. Once I write it down."

"Have you written the priest's name down?" said Omar.

The man looked at the ledger. He studied the names. He flipped a page back and studied again. "No," he said. "I haven't yet." He took up his pen and wrote down a name.

"Did you just write it down?" said Lewis.

"No," said the man. "They've got to go in order. It's very important."

"How many names till the priest's name?" said Omar.

The man looked at the boy. He still seemed very cross. He picked up the sheet of paper and studied it. He flipped back a few pages. "A long ways off yet."

"How long till you write it?"

"I don't know."

"Another hour?"

"Yes," said the man. "In another hour. If I'm left in peace, that is. I can't write down the names if I have any distractions."

"Well, we'll stay, then," said Lewis.

"No you won't," said the man.

Lewis looked at the man. "Can I have my handkerchief back?" he said.

The man picked it up and handed it across the desk. Then he set about writing down the names. He copied five names. Then ten, then twenty. The boys sat there and watched him. After a time, Omar took the bone back from the desk.

"Goodbye now," said the man.

"We're not leaving," said the boys.

The man put his pen down. He was very cross this time. More so than before. He looked at Lewis, and then at Omar. He studied the boys. They looked back at him.

"Wait here," he said.

He stood up from his desk and went back into the maze of shelves. They listened to him rummaging around in the shoes. The book was open on the desk, and the boys thought about leaning forward and reading the names again. But they didn't. They sat on the chairs and looked back where the man had gone. Every few moments, Lewis' head jerked to the side.

When the man returned he held a pair of white shoes. Leather, not sneakers. He placed them on the desk and sat down. He turned the lantern up so the boys could see. He placed his elbows on the desk and looked at Omar.

They were Omar's mother's shoes. She'd become a nurse's assistant in her last year, had been studying for it for years before that. The shoes were large and worn, and the laces were still tied up in a bow. They seemed to hover there, in the lantern light, and the boy stood up and picked up the shoes. They were heavy and warm to the touch. He sat down and held them in his lap. Often enough, she couldn't find them at home, and he'd searched under chairs and tables, in closets for them. She'd been a large woman, and he'd liked that about her. The way she might pick him up and he'd disappear.

Lewis held out the handkerchief to him, and Omar shook his head. He wiped his eyes with the sleeve of his jacket. He held the shoes in his lap until they became a white blur. He touched the laces and the rubber soles. There were strings hanging off the edge where the fabric had been worn away and he touched these gently. He thought of her name. Clara. Though he didn't say it aloud. He took the shoes up in his hands and placed them back on the desk. Back exactly where he'd taken them. Then he sat in the chair and looked up at the man.

The man had taken the handkerchief that Lewis had offered, and he was wiping his eyes. He closed the book. He looked behind the boys, as if there might be someone standing there. Someone he knew. When the boys looked, there was only the doorway and the shelves of shoes.

"That was very mean of me," said the man. "I'm very sorry about that." The man picked up the shoes and placed them in a drawer. The boys listened to the drawer shut. "It's just that I need you to leave. I know you came to see your mother's shoes, not to get the boots. I'm terribly sorry about that. It's time for you to go."

Omar looked up at him. He wiped his eyes again with his sleeve. "That's not true," he said. "We came to get the boots."

"Did you?"

"Yes," said the boy.

The man sat back in the chair. He studied the boy for a long while. The fire had ebbed, and the man looked there. It was still warm in the room. The man closed the book.

"Would you like something to drink?"

"Okay," said Omar.

The man opened a box next to the desk. "Do you like soda? Both of you?"

"Yes," they said.

"I have cola and I have lemon."

"Lemon," they said.

"I have just the one can," he said. "You'll have to share."

They said that was all right, and he took out two cups and emptied the can into them. He was very careful with the last drops. He watched the cups carefully, so there would be an equal amount in each. He passed them over to the two boys, and they drank from them. They sipped slowly. That was the polite way to do things.

"I have to go back to my work now," he said.

"How many names before the priest?" said Lewis.

"Many," said the man.

"We'll wait," said Omar.

"I'd rather that you leave," said the man.

"We'll wait," said Lewis, and his head jerked to the side.

The man opened the book. He took up the pen. He began to copy names from the paper into the book. Every few minutes he'd look up at the boys, and there they were, sipping their sodas. He put the names down carefully, and in order. He blocked the boys out of his mind.

"You don't know about waiting," he said. "I've waited here forever. Do you understand that? I've waited here since before you were born, and I'll be waiting here long after you've gone. Here. I've waited here forever. For the shoes and the boots, and especially for the names. And I will continue to wait here forever. Until all of the shoes and boots, and all of the names come in. You can't outwait me. Do you understand that? I've waited the longest. I am the longest waiter."

He looked up from his book at them. The boys stared. They seemed to stare hard at him, as if they were waiting for him to say something else. He wrote down a name, then looked back at the boys. They took a sip of soda. Swallowed. They stared back at him.

"We'll wait," they said.

The priest sat near the window and looked out at the snow. He had the blanket around him, and he pulled it close so that it covered his body up to the neck. He'd been into the wine a bit, and he'd had the shivers all night. When he closed his eyes he had a strange but familiar dream where he was sinking in deep water. There was something heavy in his pockets and it was pulling him down. The water was cold and it was dark below him. There were people above in boats, people he seemed to know, sitting and watching, though no one moved to help. The weight and the cold pulled him down and he struggled to get at the air. He breathed in and was pulled under.

When he woke, he looked out at the snow. Nothing much had changed. Saint Joseph was out there, where he always was, and the statue wore a coat of ice about his shoulders, and there was a tiny white hat of snow on his head.

The priest heard a knock at the door, and he stood up and walked across the sacristy in his stocking feet. On the ledge outside were his boots, set upright and facing the road, as if he could simply step into them. There was a cold wind, and he shivered in the doorway. Two sets of snowy footprints led away from the church. He looked out into the street, and there were two boys passing through the glow of a street-light. They were walking fast, and their hands were stuck down into their pockets. The head of the shorter boy jerked to the side. The priest picked up the boots and found a note tucked into one of the foot holes. The note was written in small block letters, though it contained no names. It asked him to please put the boots on, and near the bottom was a re-minder about a mass at nine-thirty the next morning. It was a feast day, the priest remembered now. Something very important had happened a long time ago.

We didn't ask your name, the note read. *Will you tell it to us tomorrow?* These words were crossed out once and then written again, then crossed out again, then written a third time. It seemed as if there had been a very serious discussion about content between the writers of the note. The priest looked at the bottom of the paper.

We'll be waiting for you, it read. *At nine. If it's convenient. On the back steps.*

CIRCUS NIGHT

Laika stands on her hands, watches a young elephant and its trainer, upside down, make their way slowly across the tent grounds. The elephant's trunk keeps tickling the armpit of the trainer, and the trainer swats it away, taps the straw at the ground with his short pole. The damp air smells of straw and the sweat of the circus performers. Some sour candy, baking somewhere. A tired donkey—painted in red and white stripes—is tied to a fencepost, and it watches Laika with lazy eyes, as if it is asleep and observing a dream.

A child, years younger than Laika, runs past her, and the child's dramatic costume—covered with tiny silver bells and larger pieces of crystal—seems to make an irregular song, like a wind chime or a collection of tiny clocks. The child begins to herd a group of pelicans toward their cage, and Laika, still in her handstand, shifts the weight on her arms, turns to watch, adjusts the large rubber ball at her feet, raises it toward the roof of the tent. Behind the pelicans, a pair of jugglers toss four or five torches back to one another, underhand. The woman juggler is blindfolded. The torches are not yet lit.

Laika hears heavy footsteps behind her but does not turn to see their source. She closes her eyes and listens to the sounds beyond the steps: an organ playing something bouncy and ridiculous, and the shouts of the barker practicing in front of the reptile tent. Laika can make out only a few words: A Seat at the Glass, A Few Coins in Your Pocket, Lizards Big as Men. Someone grabs her ankles and she is lifted up. She hears the ball bounce to the ground. Feels fingers at her neck, her ribs, her wrists. The blood rushes back from her head as she is lifted up, tilted horizontal, and carried away from the ring.

When she opens her eyes, she sees the top of the tent. She looks below her. Three clowns stare up. They have a tight hold of her and she cannot move. Their faces seem cruel and grim. The clowns are in makeup but not yet in costume. They say nothing as they carry Laika from the tent. Outside, the rain has stopped, and between the clouds she can see a few stars. The air is humid and warm, and the clowns slip along through the mud, cursing quite loudly, but their grips on her do not slacken. Over by the trailers, the acrobats appear—all of them standing naked—smoking cigarettes and motioning to each other with their hands as a way of speaking. She always takes note of the acrobats. Always. In the moonlight, they seem beautiful and ancient.

A flap in the animal tent is pulled back and Laika is suddenly blinded by bright orange lights. She smells must and dung, hears an annoyed horse snorting somewhere. Her chin is knocked against a support bar of the tent. When Laika complains, the three clowns look up at her briefly, and then all three say, Sorry, together, like a choir, a bit off tune. The clowns stop at a tall fence line. They toss her over the side. She's falling like she's always falling in her dreams. Laika lands in a pile of fresh straw. The albino camel, a few feet away and always temperamental, observes her, chewing his dinner sideways.

That camel—the albino camel—had spit at her only yesterday, missed by an inch or two, though Laika's face had caught the spray. Now it offers no move toward her. Its ears retreat and it sniffs the air. Laika watches the feet of the clowns as they exit the tent, more feet beyond. She offers her middle finger, and the last clown, without even looking at her, offers his in return. The tent flap drops closed, and just like that they are gone.

A long brush and a bucket drop into the straw next to her, and Laika looks up at the large frame of the tent boss. His moustache is blonde, with streaks of gray at the ends, and his dark spectacles glitter in the lamplight. He holds his tall hat in his hands, straightening the lip, and he clicks his tongue while observing her.

What's another term for indispensable? he says.

Laika is annoyed. Assistant Camel-Keeper, she says.

That's right.

She sits up in the straw. Picks up the bucket with her smallest toe. You say that about everyone.

The tent boss sets his hat on his head. But I'm lying to them.

The two boys keep the rats away with splintered wooden boards that someone had thrown down the elevator shaft. They build a wall of garbage with food and empty vials and needles, and the rats—two or three at a time—try to break through. A milk carton floats in the muck, and half a skeleton of a rat or cat is half-submerged next to it. Toomey, the younger of the two boys, stands on a burned tire near the corner of the shaft, and Eli, fourteen, pushes the rats away. The smell is terrible. They take shallow breaths and think about suffocation. Above them, the drug dealer and his men enter the elevator, and when it lowers to the bottom floor the boys kneel in the muck and try to keep their heads from being crushed in the gears.

In the second hour, and in the third, the light in the shaft begins to fade, and the roaches emerge from the walls. The boys slap at their necks and legs.

The elevator shaft door opens on the second floor and a thick beam of blue light illuminates the cinder blocks. The boys squint in the brightness and press themselves against the wall. The elevator is well above. A figure stands in the light and something heavy is tossed down. They hear it slap against the walls—a plastic bag—and tumble down the shaft. It splashes in the muck and sends the rats scrambling for the hole. Another bag follows. It just misses Toomey but breaks their wall of garbage. Two bags more. Eli closes his eyes and tries to make himself smaller, but the last bag hits him hard in the shoulder and neck. He feels something sharp, then something warm. The shaft doors close and they are left in darkness again.

Eli brushes the broken glass out of his hair, wipes the blood at his neck. They rebuild their wall and sink further into the muck.

The old woman sets the unfinished wig aside, cuts the string with scissors, and examines her finger. She'd slid it too far under the needle, and it had been drawn into the sewing machine. Her finger is jammed into the sewing machine. A line of white stitching runs up her thumb, and the blood drips into her palm, off the side of the machine, collects in a small pool on the table. But the old woman can't see much of this. She'd sewn without her glasses, which she couldn't find, and this was the result. She has a deadline for the wig, for a man across town, his hair fallen out from a harsh medicine he's been taking. She scoops the wig up in her good hand, tosses it to the counter to keep from staining it, and then she sets her face close to the damaged thumb, takes some tissues from the box next to the machine, applies some pressure to the wound.

She tugs at the lever to the needle, but her thumb has broken the machine. She sets the soaked bunch of tissues aside. The telephone, she believes, is not far from her on the counter. Where are her glasses? She dreads calling anyone she knows. She might be taken away from her house. Her house might be taken away from her. She squints and can just see the distance to the counter. She wonders if the table can be tugged that far. Her cat, Hungry, is a gray blur sitting next to the telephone.

Would you pass that over? she says.

Hungry answers with what sounds like a question in his throat.

Well, what'll happen to me if I quit? the old woman says. In a couple weeks they'll be throwing sand on my casket.

Hungry says nothing to that.

The woman sets her feet against the floor, takes the leg of the table with the good hand, pulls. An inch or two toward the counter. She scoots her chair the same distance, pulls at the table leg again.

It puts her in mind of something from decades before. She was a teenager then. She'd taken a motorboat up the Cape Fear River, though she can't now remember why. A handsome and dangerous boy upstream, likely. It was night, and in the beam of the spotlight she'd spotted a coyote swimming across the river. Its eye had burned red in the glow of the light, and it seemed both angry for the interruption and a bit frightened of drowning. As she steered around it, she could see that a pup followed the coyote, and then another after that. They bobbed in the wake of the boat and disappeared.

Laika leads the albino camel into the pen, ties it securely to a post, offers a stick of celery to keep its attention. She takes up the brush and the bucket of water, climbs up a ladder, and examines the creature's coat for the usual bugs.

Laika wants to be an acrobat more than anything in the world. In her mind she stands in the middle ring of the circus. Imagines her toes against the mat. She begins a jog, then a sprint, counts out the steps, concentrates on the vault spring. She tries to feel rather than see the pyramid of acrobats beyond. They are waiting for her to cap the top of the pyramid. When her feet tip the board her arms are tucked against her sides, legs stiff and knees loose. She vaults up, twists as gravity takes its course. She flies over the top of the pyramid. Misses it completely. Other times, in her mind, she smashes into the top row. The acrobats fall around her. There's a broken wrist and a dislocated hip, someone's eye gouged out. Worse sometimes: her own spine.

Laika can't get it right. Her head.

She sets the brush against the camel's coat, pulls down and back.

Eli steps onto Toomey's back, takes the screwdriver from his pocket, slides the blade between the doors of the elevator. The switch is popped and he opens the doors an inch, listens for any noise in the hallway. When there is nothing, he pulls the doors apart, looks down the hall.

A broken mop sits in the light of an open door. Eli pushes off Toomey, rises out of the elevator shaft, pulls his friend up after. They breathe the hallway air. Eli makes a promise to himself to never go in a place like that again, come what may.

The boys make their way quietly into the stairwell. They pause, listen, then go down the steps.

The air outside is cool now, though they can smell the stench from the sewage plant. It's an improvement over what they breathed before. They kneel on the stoop, in the shadows, and examine the back lot. Eli lets his eyes adjust to the light of the moon and a streetlamp across the wide, fast-moving river. Abandoned cars stretch across the lot. Lines of fencing. Trash of all sorts: tires and bricks, a shopping cart. An oven, half-sunk in the mud. What remains of a burned-out chimney. A roach crawls over Toomey's hand, and he shakes it free.

They see the spark of a lighter in the backseat of one of the cars. In the glow they can make out a face: a man named Baxx, one of the dealer's men. The flame goes out, and Eli surveys the rest of the lot. He listens to the wild river beyond the cars and the fencing. Somewhere, from the front of the building, he can hear a metal pipe thumping against bricks. Coming closer.

Don't stop for anything, he says.

The boys rise and run.

Johnson wipes his fist against the taxicab's windshield, makes a hole in the fog to see through. He runs the address through his mind again and watches for numbers on mailboxes, of which there are few. The road is narrow and bordered with deep gullies along each side and lined by pine trees that bow a little with the wind. He'd been sleeping in his cab, on a turnoff on the state highway. Before the call came in. Briefly, he'd had a dream where a voice had said, There's Not Enough Room, and there was a wolf, somewhere in the distance, and others approaching in the rain. Later, he felt himself begin to drown in dark water, but he couldn't make a sound. Something was pulling at his ankles, something down there in the dark, and Johnson couldn't make it let go.

When he finds the address he turns into the driveway and tries to push the dreams from his mind. He is a large man, Johnson, and he's been struggling to keep the weight off. He keeps a plastic bag of carrots in the seat next to him to keep his hunger at bay. The house is dark, although there seems to be a porch light on in back. He honks the horn, makes a notation in his logbook, and takes out a carrot. He thinks when his shift is over he might get good and drunk, although that would not be unusual. He rubs at his legs, numb from sitting in the cab so long.

Johnson eats the carrot, chews slowly, and waits. After a time, when no one comes out of the house, he honks again. He notices that the window near the front door is propped open with a wooden spoon; he can just make it out from the light of a streetlamp down the road. A broken porch swing sits out in the yard. He thinks then of something his mother often said: Much of life is not what is done simply, it's what is simply done. She had all her strange sayings, and he keeps only a few of them now. He is forty-two, and she has long since passed away.

He takes his flashlight from under the seat—Johnson has used it as a club on more than one occasion, when a passenger has tried to rob him—and he gets out of the cab. His feet slip in the mud as he makes his way up the driveway. He thinks he can hear chickens in the yard next to this one, though he can see little. When he comes to the steps, he goes up them and presses the doorbell. When there is no sound, he taps the door with the flashlight, shouts, Cab! in through the window. A dog barks from somewhere down the road.

I'll need some help with my bags, the voice, a woman's voice, inside says, and so Johnson tries the knob, lets the door swing open. He steps into the darkness and switches on the flashlight.

The house is mostly bare, with a few pictures of children on the walls and two chairs placed oddly back-to-back in the den. A coffee mug filled with pencils sits on the floor and a large black freight scale stands near an empty table. He goes into the hallway and calls Cab! again.

Down here! is the reply, and he follows the voice. He passes the bathroom and the laundry, and he enters the kitchen, where a lamp glows in the corner.

An old woman cranes her neck toward him. A few mannequin heads are set on the countertop, some bald, some not. They have no eyes, but they face toward him, all in a row. Johnson notes that they are quite creepy. The woman sits at a table next to the countertop. A cat sits in her lap, looks up at him also.

Hey, says Johnson.

Hey, says the woman. You see my glasses anywhere?

Johnson looks around. No.

Your head looks like a big potato from here.

A potato?

Maybe a squash.

Johnson looks at the woman's hand. It's caught in the stamp needle of a sewing machine. Gobs of wet tissues are set all along the table.

Did you call an ambulance?

I can't afford an ambulance. I called you. How much is a lift into town?

He thinks that over. Thirty or so.

The woman seems to think it over too. All right, she says. Give me a hand with this lever.

Johnson sets the flashlight on the counter. When he bends at the table, the cat jumps off the woman's lap and sniffs his shoes. He examines the needle, and the woman points at the lever above it.

Just one good yank, she says.

Not sure if I'm equipped.

Don't be a ninny, says the woman. I've got the hard part.

Johnson sets one of his thick hands against the tabletop and with the other he takes the lever. He nudges the cat away with the toe of his shoe. Then he pulls the lever up, slowly. The woman makes no sound. When her thumb comes free, she holds it up to the lamplight, and Johnson picks up a dishtowel from the sink, runs some water over it. The woman's glasses are next to the sink, and he picks them up as well.

Here, he says, and he sets the eyeglasses on her face, hands her the dishtowel. She looks up at him.

You don't look like a potato at all.

Thanks, he says. You want some help out?

I could probably make it. What kind of help you offering?

I'd have to pick you up, he says.

That might be nice.

So he pulls her chair back from the table and slips his arms under her knees and around her back. When he lifts her up, she feels like a small stack of blankets.

I won't drip on your shirt, she says.

He takes the flashlight from the counter and maneuvers his way out of the kitchen and into the hallway. She reaches over, turns on the light for him. The dishtowel is stained red, and the old woman has a streak of blood in her hair where she brushed it back.

When they come to the den, Johnson looks at the two chairs. Their backs are pressed against each other and they face away, as if two invisible sitters are in argument.

Why are they turned like that? he says.

The chairs?

Yes.

When I'm thinking about writing a letter I look out the window, she says. When I write it, I face the wall.

He nods at the freight scale. And that?

My father's. He owned a vegetable store. Years ago, I guess. They'd sell by bulk.

It's still accurate?

I suppose.

Johnson steps into the den, switches his flashlight on. The cat has followed them in, and it watches as Johnson steps up onto the scale. He shines the light at the reading.

How much you weigh? he says.

About eighty.

He checks the reading again. Subtracts the woman's weight from what he reads. He shifts the woman a little higher in his arms, watches for any movement in the needle. Those carrots don't seem to be helping. He frowns and exhales.

Laika stands under the bright yellow and blood–colored lights outside the reptile tent. She holds a coffee mug filled with potato soup, and she spoons it, blows the steam away, takes another taste. The circus has opened, and she watches a small group of children form an attentive semicircle around the jugglers. The jugglers' torches are now lit, and the blindfolded pair toss the flames underhanded while black smoke curls in the air. The children turn their heads back and forth then back again, following the flames. On a stand near the center of the tent, the organist plays the same ridiculous tune, and behind him, a clown stands with a pail of water.

Laika walks through the crowd, tries to keep the soup from spilling. In the main ring, a woman with dark, curled hair balances atop one of the jogging elephants. The woman has always put Laika in mind of her mother. The crowd is seated in stands on three sides, and there are orange glow-sticks here and there, a pair of children holding sparklers. Around and around the ring the elephant goes, and the woman sets her hands against the creature's thick back, handstands, points her long legs at the roof of the tent. The acrobat leans in to keep from falling. The crystals in her costume catch the spotlights, and around she goes again, glittering like a figure in water. The elephant trudges on, looking, unlike many of the animals, happy to be of service.

From somewhere Laika hears a barker. She imagines the man's hand sweeping above the crowd. I Have a Number for You Sir. And I Believe It's a Winner. In six hours, well after the circus closes, Laika will find the acrobats again, will unbraid the dark curled hair of the woman, will rub away the knots in her shoulders. When the woman needs a brief affection—she often seems to—Laika will hold her hand.

And of course Laika will think about her mother, who, years before—almost five now—had passed her between lines of barbed wire. A man and his wife were waiting in darkness on the other side. Laika, as a young child, had left the refugee camp that way. They were many miles outside Sarajevo. The floodlights were out then, and the soldiers were standing at the gates.

If the rain holds off this night, Laika and the woman will sit near the bonfire—the bonfire after most circus nights, and there might be a boy—the giant's son—who Laika wouldn't mind speaking with again. There is something that she finds delightful about the giant's son that she can neither understand nor explain. The boy had taken her out to the tracks the morning before. He'd set his head against the rails, looked up at her. You can hear them coming, he'd said, but when she knelt next to him she'd heard nothing. The cold metal had sent a shiver through her ear that ran down her arms to her fingertips.

She checks her watch, finishes her potato soup. She slips down a space next to the reptile tent, watches for snakes in the straw. They often escape. Above her, she watches a monkey on the tightwire. It swings by its hands across the wire to a bell, which the creature rings with a thump of its fingertip. Then, back across. The floor is twenty feet down, and when the monkey returns to the stand, it is rewarded with a piece of fruit from its keeper.

Out through the back of the tent and up the hill past the trailers. Laika looks up at the leaden sky and thinks she can see some shapes in the clouds. A man with no arm in that one. The broken tip of a javelin in that one. A giant eye that can see everything but her. She is not without some skills: past the trailers she finds an open space, does her cartwheels and then a running tumble, lands on her feet, and then tumbles again. The hand walk is simple to her, even in the mud, and she sets herself on both arms, turns with a slight movement of the fingers, watches the upside down hooves of the horses in the animal tent.

She opens the flap with her feet, walks into the light, her palms and fingers pressed against the straw and the dung. Her shadow is clear in the lamp glow, an upside-down girl, but she can't seem to see herself in it. She imagines it as maybe belonging to another girl from somewhere far off. Maybe someone with her face, but a different name. The wire gate to the camel pen looks, from her angle, to be open, so she closes her eyes and breathes in deep: it gives her a buzz with all that blood in her head.

Then, she falls over and gets up quickly. Another rush. She looks at the gate, and again it seems open. That couldn't possibly be. She scans the pen for the white camel, the rare and expensive camel, the camel that she alone is responsible for and to. Laika runs into the pen and searches every corner, every possible hiding place. There is no hiding place here for a camel of that size. Here there is only straw.

Toomey slips in the mud and topples into a line of wire. It tangles his shirt, his jeans. He can't get free of it. Baxx is out of the car and shouts back toward the building, and Eli pulls the wire free, pulls the younger boy up, gives him a shove toward the river. They desperately want to get to the other side of the fast-moving river. They watch Baxx try to cut off their angle to the water.

Toomey heads away from the chimney and toward the fence. The dark water of the river is twenty yards ahead of him, and he scrambles over what is left of a couch, takes the back end like a hurdle, hears Eli close behind, sees Baxx bearing down on them. At the river bank the boy jumps, feet first, and lands in water to his kneecaps. His spine runs a lightning chill, and he pushes out and dives.

He tastes gasoline. It sears the back of his throat, stings his eyes. The shock of the cold water pushes him on. He comes up for air, and he can feel the current pushing him quickly south. He turns, looks behind at two shadows, a man and a boy. The boy dives, and the man falls back into the bank, sinks to his knees. A screwdriver is stuck through the man's palm. Behind him, two figures run in shadow toward the river. The water rises, and Toomey goes under.

He lets the swift current take him away from the men, out to where the water becomes sudden deep. His shoes kick against nothing. Surfacing, he catches a glimpse of the far bank—mud and shallows—and he makes for it. He kicks through the cold water. Under the surface he thinks of Eli, and above it he thinks of his own drowning. He chokes on the gas water. The fumes begin, it seems, to trick his vision. He's almost to the far bank, but the water moves there in a strange way. He pushes down and his shoes find mud and shallow water.

The first of the rats. Claws and tails. Teeth. They hook to his arm and he shakes them free. Feels one at his neck, and then he's in the thick of them. He sweeps them heavily aside, chokes on the gas again. He falls in the shallows, and they're upon him. Toomey gets up, moves forward. He finds the bank and comes free of the water.

He steps on the rats, trips, falls in the mud and broken crates, feels a nail stick into his knee. It goes in deep, and when he raises the leg a board is stuck there. He can't bend his leg. He takes hold of the board. A gunshot behind him. He pulls the board out, pulls it free, cries the pain out of himself. The knee goes numb. He hits the rats with the board, and then he's up the muddy bank. He looks back for Eli. Looks for what the moonlight will offer. The men are climbing a fence on the other side of the river. The current has taken him far downstream. A boy surfaces in the shallows below, and Toomey stumbles down the bank. He takes the collar of the boy who kneels in the shallows, choking.

Over the bank and into a ditch. No rats there, only broken pipes and some beer bottles, a box of diapers sunk into the mud. The boys spit poison from their mouths. Their lungs are like fire. They listen to the river, they try to stay alive. When he catches a clean breath, Toomey feels at his knee. There's a sick-feeling hole there.

They lie in the ditch and look up at the sky. They don't have the energy yet to move, though they can hear the shouts of the dealer and his men across the river. The stars are out, and Toomey sees them as bits of blue. He looks for the moon but can't yet find it.

They coming? he says, and Eli raises his head. The boy picks up a length of pipe and crawls slowly up the ditch. Toomey can see his head poke up into the clearing.

They wait. One boy watches and the other boy listens. When Eli climbs down he looks at his friend. He has a smile on his face.

They can't swim, he says.

Johnson drives the taxi slowly, passes the turn for the state highway. Next to him, the old woman holds her bad arm with the good hand, tries to keep it elevated. Johnson has a sister, Marley, a nurse. He thinks maybe she can help this woman out. He'll skirt the city, near the old fairgrounds, and head up to her house. A farm on the other side of town. Above them the sky has cleared of clouds, and the moon shines through the tree line. It puts Johnson in mind of a girl he'd once known. She'd had a penchant for climbing things: trees and rooftops, a billboard for a hotel chain near where he'd grown up. He was afraid of heights himself, but he often, as a child, found himself waiting on her. He feels the crick in his neck now, from staring up all those years ago.

You didn't put the meter on, says the woman. I like to pay for what I owe.

He thinks on that but doesn't argue. He pulls the lever down. They listen to the ticks as they make their way down the road.

These carrots yours? says the woman.

Who else?

I'll give you two dollars for them.

You can just have them, he says.

I need them for tomorrow. I have a donkey to feed. Will you take two dollars for them?

Johnson looks over at the carrots. I didn't see a barn at your house.

My sister owns one. She lives in a nursing home just south of here.

Johnson reaches over, takes the woman's arm. Holds it up. You can rest that awhile if you want.

A minute, says the woman.

Johnson nods. She's got a donkey in a nursing home?

Not really. My sister's a little far gone. She thinks she's got this donkey named Nelson. They keep him in a shed out back.

You feed him?

Three times a week, the woman says.

What about the other days?

I don't think she keeps track, and besides, she can't get up and around very well, so whenever I visit I bring some vegetables for Nelson. He's very particular. He eats mustard greens. You have any of those around here?

No, says Johnson.

You ever hear of a donkey eating something like that?

I haven't heard much about donkeys at all.

He'll eat alfalfa and carrots, says the woman. But he gets awfully irritable if I give him celery. He seems to like corn, though.

Johnson looks over at her. Sounds like you're the one a little far gone.

Maybe, says the woman. You'd not be the first to make the claim. You want to hear something else?

All right.

There's a red-handled brush. It's soft. Nelson likes to be brushed with that. If you brush him with one of the others, he doesn't like it.

They come to a four-way stop, and Johnson gives the woman her arm back. He slows the cab and looks for traffic. There's nothing, though, just empty tobacco fields and an old tractor, set near a wire fence. The moonlight reflects off the tire hub, and they smell fertilizer and the dusty crops through the open windows. They hear the whistle of a train in the distance, though they can't see it. Johnson pushes on through the intersection.

Sounds like this donkey's particular, he offers.

That's not the half of it, says the old woman. He likes to walk counterclockwise around the shed and the yard. If you walk him clockwise, he can't sleep at night. And then you've got to keep him from the roosters. They'll peck at his legs, and he'll kick the hell out of them. Then you've got a dead rooster on your hands, and what's that good for?

Johnson considers that. I can't think of anything, he says.

And you've got to get his blanket on anytime it's going to drop below forty degrees. He'll catch a cold otherwise. You walk out past the water pump—a yellow one—but that hasn't worked for years, and the shed is after that. The latch is tricky, though. You've got to push on the door, or else it won't open. There's a man who lives in the home with my sister, and he's always asking me how to work that latch.

Johnson looks over at the woman. Johnson doesn't consider himself a master of conversation. This sounds complicated, he says.

Well, all I really do is walk outside and stand on the porch for about a half hour. But sometimes it takes me a long time to think up a new story about Nelson. If I don't have something new, my sister gets upset.

Johnson takes up her arm again, lets her rest the good one.

I'd guess that means a lot to her, he says.

Maybe. She's pretty far gone. It's kind of sad really. Feeding an imaginary donkey. They'll likely be locking me up next. Do we have a deal for the carrots?

Sure, says Johnson. How's the finger?

The woman looks there. She tries to wiggle it a little under the dishcloth.

It might be I'll lose it.

Laika makes her way downhill through the strangleweed. Behind her, the lights and sounds of the circus begin to fade. The camel is down in a large meadow, not far from the tree line, and it looks like a strange little ghost at this distance. Beyond it, and beyond the trees, Laika can see a two-lane road. A few cars moving in either direction. She finds her footing in the rocks and the mud. At the bottom of the hill she smells the wet grass and sweetness of the yellow flowers that stretch across the field. Through the center, she can see the tracks that the camel stamped through the flowers. Bats circle the fields above her, and the sounds of the night bugs are loud in the valley, all along the hillsides.

She keeps low as she pushes through the flowers. The camel eyes her from the field. A thick rope hangs from below its jaw, and the twine stretches across the ground like a long water serpent. She imagines it in the reptile tent. And then she looks up at the stars and the moon, and they put her in mind of a march she'd made as a child. Days after she'd been passed through the barbed wire. She'd held onto an old man's hand, and the man had guided her through a stretch of fields not unlike this one. As they reached the mountains, she'd become the guide to him. She'd pushed him forward and up during that night. All the night.

Behind them, they could hear the mortar shells, and the hooves of horses along the road. Another woman—the old man's wife—walked ahead of them, and every few minutes she'd turn and look down at them. She held the hands of two other children. You'll make it, she'd said, although she'd not spoken any words. It was the expression in the woman's face that seemed to say that for her.

Laika, now, can't remember either of their names. But she sees their faces very clearly.

When she comes almost free of the flowers she slows, begins to whisper to the camel in tones meant to soothe. Her voice is not insincere. The camel points its ears forward, studies her, as if with a little effort it might make out the words. Its tail snaps at the few bugs that have found its coat. Laika is almost within spitting distance by then—the camel's spitting distance, not hers—and she keeps her eyes on the rope. A few steps and a dive and she might have it. But the camel begins to move, backing up toward the tree line. Laika quickens her pace, and the creature turns—they are not without speed—and sets off in the direction of the road. Laika runs after it. She cuts through the flowers. The rope trails behind, and Laika smells the must and fur of the creature. She dives then, reaches out for the twine, and catches it near the end. She clamps one hand over the other. But the camel pushes on. When the line snaps taut, it whips through the palm of her hand, tearing the skin. The knot slips through her fingers, and she watches it skip across the grass and mud.

She sits up. Examines the burn on her hand. No blood, but it's hot to the touch. She spits into it, rubs it cool. What were their names? The man and his wife. She thinks of her mother's name. Whispers it to the bats above her. She stands up, rubs what mud she can manage off her clothes. She was very angry a moment ago, but now that has passed and has passed for the night. She follows the creature—jogging, then running—out toward the road.

The boys smell of sewer and gasoline as they make their way along the ditch. They have a good start to the train yard, and they pause at the edge of the field to wash their hair and faces in mud water. Eli cleans out the puncture in Toomey's knee, ties one of his socks around the wound. After, the younger boy leans heavily against him, and they take the quickest pace they can manage. Their eyes, still stung by gasoline, won't stop dripping tears.

At the rail yard they find a hole in the fence and sit under an abandoned boxcar. They keep watch, down toward the tracks. Eli finds a wooden stake, keeps it between his fingers, digs down into the mud. They look behind often, waiting and worrying. They think they can see men with pipes and long chains in the shadows, and then they blink them away. The shadows take another form. In the rail yard, a pair of figures stands between a locomotive and a tanker car. The workmen check the connection.

After a time, the sky begins to drizzle. The boys listen to the rainwater. It trickles off the side of the boxcar.

I'm hungry for some pizza, says Toomey.

Eli frowns at that. What're you telling me for?

No one else around.

Eli says nothing to that.

Toomey looks behind them. With some chicken and potatoes, and extra cheese.

We'll maybe get some potatoes tomorrow, says Eli. You'll have to imagine the rest.

And some soda.

Water, says Eli.

And some bread sticks.

Bread, no sticks.

And some ice cream, says Toomey.

All right.

Really?

No.

What're you teasing me for?

Eli shrugs. No one else around.

Down by the tracks, Eli can see a workman open the gates. The boy crawls to the boxcar wheel. He finds another pool of mud water, and he washes his eyes again. He works the plan in his head, not for the train but beyond it.

I heard Jenna downstairs, says Toomey.

Eli looks back at him. I know, Toomey.

So I went down there.

Well, you shouldn't have. They could've killed you too.

The fire escape, says Toomey. Like you showed me. I could see them through the window. She wasn't dead yet.

Eli looks out at the train. He says nothing.

She was my friend, says Toomey.

I know.

Where's that train go?

How would I know? Out of here, I guess. Keep quiet now.

They wait after that, watch the two figures under the lamplight. The two men share a cigarette. One of them writes something on a clipboard. Eli had lived once, out there, where the train might go. His grandfather. It seems like a long time ago, but it's only a year. The train begins to move.

They watch the boxcars pass, and the tankers after. It's a long line. The whistle blows, and Toomey covers his ears. It takes Eli from his thoughts. He'd almost found the face of his grandfather in his mind.

You ready? he says.

Toomey says nothing.

Eli waits for the whistle to stop, then he takes the boy's hands from his ears.

You ready?

They messed her up bad.

I know, says Eli.

They rise and run. They run past the two men and they run out past the gate. Eli takes Toomey's weight on, slips the boy's arm around his shoulders. There's a naked woman there, by the side of the tracks, sitting in a pile of cardboard boxes. They pass her and run after the train.

Marley sets the old woman's hand under a lamp light, examines the wound. Her brother Johnson sits in the corner, sipping at the last beer in her refrigerator. They listen to the old appliance now, the motor rattling in the next room. She slips out her kit from a desk drawer, pokes through the bottles and the gauze pads. She finds a plastic bag of syringes near the bottom.

This'll be your second needle of the day, she says.

The old woman smiles, polite, takes the glasses from her face. She sets them on the table, looks away so as not to see.

Tell me something, she says. To keep my mind off it.

She says this to Johnson, who stares blankly at nothing in particular. The chair beneath him is small. Unstable under his weight. He sets his hand against the windowsill for some leverage.

I got nothing, he says.

Tell her a baseball story, says Marley. She sets the needle into the rubber tip of one of the bottles, draws the solution out.

That's all a blur, he says.

He used to play, says Marley. Did he tell you that?

No, says the old woman. She feels the needle sink into her finger, just below the knuckle. She moves it from her mind. Where?

In Virginia, says Johnson. Double-A ball.

Position?

Pitcher, he says.

What was your ERA?

Johnson says nothing, chances a look over at her.

I know some things, she says.

I don't doubt that.

What was it?

It was through the roof, he says.

Hmm.

Not always, Marley says. Later, maybe.

Later was what counted, Johnson says. Let's not talk about that.

Marley slips the needle out, sets the syringe aside. He had a sinker no one could hit.

What else? says the old woman.

Johnson shrugs. I could field some. You get a pitcher who can field, you'll win some games.

Marley pours alcohol onto one of the gauze pads. She begins to clean the wound. The old woman tightens up, sits forward.

This stings, says Marley.

That's not a lie, says the old woman.

Marley reaches up, adjusts the light. She points it at her brother.

He was quite good, she says. I thought so, anyways.

Johnson squints, holds his hand up against the glow.

You have to say that. You're my sister.

She keeps the light there, and both women watch him for a while. He ignores them, looks out the window. His cab is parked at the curb. He'll make no money tonight.

Eventually, Marley turns the light back toward the old woman's hand. Some things can't be helped, she says.

In the night, the train passes on toward farmland, and Eli sits at the edge of the flatbed and looks out into the darkness. Fields and silos mostly, a small herd of goats staring out at the train. Stretches of tree line border each property. Toomey is asleep under a tarp. His head rests against a bundle of pipes, and below them the heavy wheels rattle against the tracks. The air smells of axle grease from the train and wet hay from the fields. It puts Eli in mind of another train he'd once taken. He'd seen a coyote from the window once, and another boy in a trailer park that he remembers now. His own age. The boy was balanced on an old tire, like a carnival performer. He'd waved at the train as it passed, and Eli imagined that the boy was waving at him. He'd tried to figure what the boy had seen and felt: windows black with the night, the breeze as the train passed. The boy had worn a cap backward and had no shoes on. Eli had leaned into the window, watched the boy until he was almost out of sight. He waited for the tumble to earth that did not come.

He remembers a white church on a hill. Power lines that stretched for miles. The long lake like an ocean. Tugs and barges off the shoreline. On this train they pass a cemetery, and Eli holds his breath for the distance: a trick he'd learned from his grandfather. It was for luck, and to keep spirits away. Eli takes off his wet shoes and the wet socks after. He sticks his feet over the side of the flatbed. In the distance he sees what might be a town. The tall shape of grain elevators. Trailers after that, not unlike the park with the boy on the tire, but Eli sees no movement at this hour. Just the clotheslines and a dog asleep under a tree. Sets of chairs and benches here and there. A grill made of bricks, and a flagpole with no flag. He listens to the knock of the pipes and the whistle of air from beneath the tarp. Above him, the dark power lines cross over the track.

After the next stretch of tree line he can make out the shape of a girl. She walks down from the road, into an abandoned field. There is something in the field, and it picks up the brightness of the moonlight. It looks like it might be a strange type of horse. The girl approaches it slowly. Eli thinks her rather elegant, composed, the way she moves down the hill. He can't see her face, but he imagines it. He likes this about trains. About motion and distance: what you can see and what you can't. The details you fill in, if you take the time. He imagines the eyebrows, the angle of the nose, the lines in the brow, if there are any. Motion is the thing, he believes. The space between leaving and arriving. The girl disappears from view, and he sees nothing but trees on the horizon. He tries to burn her picture into his mind.

The train turns west.

At about the same time, there is a woman—ancient by any standard Eli would choose—sleeping next to a baseball pitcher in a cab. The pitcher keeps a finger on the base of the steering wheel, crooks his elbow out the window. The man is troubled, though not by his passenger or the road before him. He hears nothing but the wind at his ears. He drives fast, though he is not in a hurry. The speed of the cab is something to lean against. They dip into farmland. Much passes by him this night, though he takes in little. He keeps his eyes on what the headlights will show. It all seems the same to Johnson.

He wonders sometimes why he feels defeated, at any time of the day, and before any task. It's like he's injured or broken before the competition begins. Was it always that way? He remembers an odd mix of images. The girl who was always climbing things. It was two girls, honestly. His sister Marley and the other girl with her. The one he loved with everything he had. He remembers that he once possessed something to lose. As he stared up at them, the sky seemed like the ocean to him, deep and dark and true. That summer there was an article in the newspaper about a manatee, a strange creature that had migrated north and would often nap in the warm outflow of a power plant. He'd scissored the article from the paper, thumbtacked it deep into the bedroom wall. The manatee was caught up in fishing nets at the end of the summer, drowned a few inches from air. That loss was amazingly present to him, like his spirit ripped through his chest bone. He wishes he could feel that way, any way, again. But he's too frightened of those feelings anymore. He doesn't know where to begin.

He listens to the wind through the car window. Another day, that same summer, he and the girl, out in the surf, out past the surf, way out there, holding hands. One was tall and they were both young. People were calling them back in, but they refused to return.

Johnson presses his foot against the brake, slows the cab at a bend in the road. Up around the next curve he can make out a girl near the shoulder of the road, her figure appearing like a kindly and benevolent ghost. When the headlights reach her, she simply squints at the brightness. She holds a rope, and—very odd—a white camel trots slowly behind her, its head hung low, picking at something on the back of girl's shirt. Johnson moves over the line in the road, gives them some room, passes them by, wonders if the woman next to him is still breathing. He slows the cab, watches her for movement.

After the cab has passed, Laika lets her eyes adjust. She lets the camel set the pace. There is no hurry, at this hour, to return. She kicks a pebble up the road and thinks of the bonfire. Just over the next hill, she hopes. The acrobat's hair, the motion of the braids she'll make, and the boy who'd set his head at the tracks. She's afraid of the giant. Laika. But likes his son. She remembers two names now. She whispers them to the camel. Old woman, old man. The camel takes no notice. One or both would reach down with fingers. Up, they'd say to her. Up and up. She gives a tug on the rope. She can allow a slow pace for only so long. The white camel tugs back, and loses. Don't spit on me, says the girl, and it does not. It trots, reluctantly, and not ungracefully, after.

GROUNDSKEEPING

It was the day after my fourteenth birthday, and I'd been looking out the window of the bus for most of Tennessee and into the Appalachians, watching the fog rise from the shoulder of the road and the patchwork of barns and homes near the state highway. A pale, spotted horse here, a brown dog lying on its side there, a group of young girls, about my age, dancing to music from a tape player set on the hood of a car. When we pulled into the station I spotted my Uncle Jake—dressed in a blue T-shirt and jeans—leaning against one of the support poles. I recognized the wide green eyes from a picture my dad kept on our mantle at home. In the picture, my dad is propped on the trunk of a yellowing Ford Pinto, a serious, solemn look on his face, even as a boy—the dark curly hair, like mine, falling down his temples—and Jake is leaning back on the fender of the car, a slight, wild grin curving from his lips, a cigarette dangling from his fingers at age fifteen. The bus driver swung open the door and called out, "Morganton. Five-minute stop," but even as I stepped across the legs of the man sitting next to me, I noticed I was the only one exiting the bus.

I stepped down onto the platform and felt the heat of the July sun. Jake ambled over and reached for the small duffel bag in my hand, but I said, "I got it."

"Is that all you got?"

"That's all I got," I said.

"Well all right then," said Jake.

His transportation was a blue flatbed pickup truck, rusted on the fenders, with a dent in the passenger-side door. In the cab of the truck I was introduced to Mulligan, a sandy-colored, overweight mutt with four white paws, like boots. Mulligan scooted to the middle of seat and sniffed at my duffel bag.

"He's got a tick in his ear," I said to Jake as I closed the door. "It's been there for a few days."

"Is that right?" Jake said, turning the key, but no sound came from the motor. He reached under the seat and pulled out a long-stem hammer, popped the hood, and got back out of the truck.

While he was banging on the starter in the engine I took out the tweezers from my pocketknife and picked up the book of matches lying on the dashboard. I lit one, letting it burn for a moment. Mulligan sniffed at the sulfur in the air. When I blew the match out I stuck it quickly to the tick, yellow and fat, its legs shuddering as I grabbed hold of Mulligan's orange collar and said, "Take it easy." I clamped the tweezers shut near the head of the tick, squeezing and prying it loose as quick as I could and then tossing it out the window with the match. Mulligan glanced sideways at me, wrinkling the white stripe of fur that ran down his snout.

When the motor turned over, Jake backed out onto a two-lane road and ran his fingers along the dashboard, eventually giving up and punching the cigarette lighter on the console. "How was the trip?" he asked.

"Long. Boring," I said.

"Did you read your books?"

"I did."

"I hear you're a big reader."

"You heard right."

"What'd you read?"

"A book about mountain climbing and a book about sharks."

"Are you a mountain climber?"

"No."

"I caught a shark on the Outer Banks last summer," he said. "Hooked him with a spring rod. Three and a half feet. A mako." The cigarette lighter popped out and Jake lit up without taking his eyes off the road.

"Makos aren't found on the Outer Banks. They're only found in warm climates."

"This was summertime," he said.

"Summer isn't warm enough. It was probably a nurse shark. They're harmless and are an endangered species."

"A nurse shark you say?"

"That's right."

"How do you know?"

"When we get to the house I'll take a look."

"What makes you think I've got it at the house?" he said.

Mulligan leaned against me as we took a turn. I looked over at Jake. "You seem like the kind of guy who would have the one shark he ever caught stuffed and put up over his mantel."

"I don't have a mantel," said Jake.

"Do you have a stuffed shark on the wall?"

"Yes I do."

"It's a nurse shark."

"You want to bet?"

"No," I said.

"You afraid of losing?"

"No, I don't bet, that's all."

"A betting man is a man who knows what he's talking about," he said. "You sound like you know what you're talking about. Why don't you take the bet?"

I looked over at him. "My dad said you once lost a house in a poker game."

Jake puffed on his cigarette and flicked the ashes out the window. "He did, did he?"

"Yes, he did."

"Well," he said. "You shouldn't believe everything you hear."

"My dad wasn't a liar."

"I didn't say he was."

"Yes you did. You just said it."

"When did I say it?"

"You implied it."

"Oh," said Jake. "I implied it."

The truck was in need of new shocks and bounced at every slight pot-hole and bump. We drifted down an off-ramp and onto a state highway, still two lanes.

"Your dad was a good man," said Jake. "But he and I were not that close."

I didn't say anything.

"How long you staying?"

"Until I hear from my mom."

"How long's that going to be?" he said.

"Not long."

Jake rubbed his hand along the wheel. "Well, I've got some rules that I want you to know about."

"You do?"

"Yes," he said. "I do."

On the highway we passed the Bonds Motel, a long brown building with an empty swimming pool. Stands with signs for homemade honey and fresh vegetables appeared every quarter mile or so, and a brick building advertising violin repair. Mulligan sat down on his haunches, licked his paw, and rubbed at the ear where the tick had been.

I asked Jake if he was going to tell me what these rules were. I told him my psychic powers weren't too good.

"Your dad was a smart-ass too," said Jake.

"Better than being a dumb-ass," I said.

Jake laughed, his white-stubbled jaw reaching forward, blowing smoke out his mouth. "I taught him that one," he said. "Better than being a dumb-ass."

"You must be real proud," I said.

"Rule one," said Jake. "I watch a lot of TV. If you don't like what I'm watching, then too bad. In my house, I'm in charge of the remote."

"I don't watch TV," I said.

"Well I guess that won't be a problem."

"Guess not."

"Well all right then," he said.

"Okay then," I said.

"Rule two," he said. "I need my sleep. I've got to be at the ballpark at 8 a.m., so no making loud noises in the middle of the night."

"I don't make loud noises in the middle of the night."

"Well I guess it won't be a problem."

"I guess not."

"Rule three," he said. "If you break something, you pay for it."

I asked him if he was running an antique shop.

"No, I'm just saying. Don't go breaking my things."

"I won't."

"Rule four," he said, rubbing his hands back and forth along the steering wheel. He flicked the ashes from his cigarette out the window again. Outside on the road we passed a veterinarian clinic and a stretch of farmland, silos and gray barns cluttered together. Jake leaned back in the seat and glanced over at me. "Well," he said. "I can't think of anything. I guess there is no number four."

"I've got some rules too," I said.

"You do?"

"I do."

"Well let's hear them."

"First," I said. "You want to smoke, then that's your prerogative, but there's the issue of secondary smoke. I don't want you bringing your cigarettes into my room, and I want the door to my room kept closed."

"Who says you're getting a room?" he said.

"I just got off a three-day bus ride. I better have a room."

Jake turned the wheel at exit 20 and gunned the engine up the on-ramp. Outside, the clouds had covered the sun.

"Did you know," I said. "A smoker can quit after seven years, and in seven more years he can have lungs that are as healthy as a person who's never smoked."

"Is that a fact?"

"I read it," I said. "It doesn't make it a fact. There are some exceptions, but for most people, that's the case."

"I see."

"How long have you smoked for?"

"Thirty-three years."

I rolled down the window to get at some air. "You're screwed," I said. "That makes you at least forty-eight years old."

"How do you figure?"

"Am I right?"

"I'll be fifty this December."

"If you make it to December," I said.

"Uh-huh," he said and flicked ashes out the window.

"Second," I said. "I don't have much stuff, but what I have I don't want you looking through. I've got a letter from my dad to you. I'll give you that when we get home."

"What's it say?"

"I don't know," I said. "He told me if anything ever happened to him I was supposed to give it to you."

"And you never looked at it?"

"No," I said. "It wasn't for me, it's for you."

"What do you have that you don't want me to look at?"

"Nothing," I said. "What I've got is mostly clothes and books."

"I don't read too much," he said.

"Then I guess it won't be a problem."

"I guess not."

"Well all right then."

"Okay then," he said. "You got any more rules?"

The cab of the truck bounced as we hit a pothole, and Mulligan placed his paw on my leg. "Not that I can think of," I said. "But I may come up with some more later."

"Me too," Jake said. "I may come up with some more later, too."

We turned onto a gravel driveway, covered overtop with the arching limbs of pine trees. The truck continued to bounce and lean as we made our way to the house, a wooden A-frame with a chimney, blackened at the top, and a rail-less porch on the second story. Mulligan wagged his tail and turned to look at Jake.

"This is home," Jake said.

"If you say so," I said.

The spotlights in Memorial Stadium can be seen just over the treetops on Highway 64, right next to the scoreboard with the big sign for Coca-Cola. When I arrived in mid-season, the Morganton Knights were eleven and a half games out of first place in the South Atlantic League and not looking to move up anytime soon. I'll say this for Jake: he kept a good field. The grass in the outfield was bright green, and he kept the base-lines razor-straight, not allowing the dirt to form a lip into the infield diamond. Somehow he conned some local kids into dragging the base-lines with rakes in the middle of the fifth inning, and on the nights when it rained—which was often—the Knights players themselves helped pull the light blue tarp over the dirt on the pitcher's mound and around the base paths.

I got ten dollars to mow the outfield three times a week, alternating between the 305 (the distance between the foul poles) and the checker-board cut, plus another two bucks to make sure the lime was dropped on the baselines before each game.

The second week I was there, the team mascot—some teenager dressed up in a suit of armor, no joke—passed out from heat exhaustion during the seventh-inning stretch. We could hear him clatter to the ground next to the concession stand. After the games, Jake and I dragged the infield again and he ran his hands through the grass, testing for soft spots. The night before a home stretch against Gastonia he flipped the floodlights off in the stadium and carried a lantern and a shovel in a wheelbarrow out to first base. I knelt with him in the dirt.

"The Cougars've got this kid named Ellis," he said. "He's stolen everything this year except the catcher's underwear, but we're going to fix him good."

He pitched the shovel into the ground and scooped out the topsoil where a runner would take a lead off first base. Down in its place he put a mixture of peat moss, water, and sand. Then he covered it with a thin layer of topsoil, slapping it flat with the back of the shovel. "When your man digs his cleats in here, he's going to sink like the *Lusitania*."

"Is this legal?" I asked.

"If no one finds out about it."

"It's cheating," I said.

"Well," said Jake. "You could call it that. You could also call it 'home-field advantage.'" For good measure he slanted the baselines around home plate so that any bunted ball would curve straight to the pitcher.

Some nights we took turns hitting soft loopers into the outfield, with Mulligan running out into the dark to retrieve them.

"You're not a bad hitter," said Jake after I slapped the ball, off a bounce, against the yellow-and-blue Denny's sign in left field. That was weeks later, after he'd shown me how to stand in the batter's box and dig my right foot into the dirt. "Choke up on the bat," he said. "When you get older and your arms bulk up you can grab it at the bottom. There's no shame in doing what works. You're not going to be Hank Aaron in two weeks."

"Who's Hank Aaron?" I said, but I knew.

"Jesus," said Jake, and pitched a fastball smack over home plate.

When it was his turn to bat he could smack the ball into either corner of the field—triple territory—and a few times he'd knock it over the wall. My sense was that Jake held back some. We didn't have too many baseballs to spare.

If it was late enough at night, after we collected the equipment and put it away in the shed, and after Jake walked the field one last time, plugging holes in the batter's box and pitcher's mound with wet clay from a tin bucket, then he'd push the driver's seat in the pickup truck forward and let me drive home. We never saw a police car on the back roads. Most nights I had to smack the starter with the hammer two or three times to get the engine to turn over, and then I'd let out the clutch gently and back out of the lot.

"Did you get the emergency brake?" said Jake.

"I did."

"I didn't see you do it."

"You weren't watching close enough."

The breeze slanting through the windows was cold at night, even into late July, and I kept the speedometer needle steady at forty or forty-five. After a time or two, Jake just leaned back in the passenger seat and pushed his baseball cap over his eyes. Mulligan sat across him with his head out the window. Every few minutes Jake stretched his legs out in the cab and I could hear the *pop-pop* of his kneecaps and hear him sigh in relief.

"Your mom's got my number?" said Jake.

"She does."

"You told her you were staying here?"

"I didn't talk to her," I said. "I told her neighbor on the phone, and he said he'd give her the message."

"Your mom still in that hospital?"

"What do you know about it?"

"I don't know anything except what your dad told me in the letter."

"What'd he say in the letter?"

He flipped the cap up over his eyes and looked out the windshield. "The turn's coming up here."

"I know where it is."

"Why haven't you asked me about the letter before now?"

"Because," I said, "the letter was for you. I try to stay out of people's business."

Jake nodded. "That you do."

"You don't have to tell me if you don't want to."

"I'll tell you."

I glanced over at him. "Well what are you waiting for then?"

He looked out on the road. "I'm waiting for you to make this turn up here that we're going too fast to make."

I pressed down on the brake and made the turn. A sedan in the other lane stopped as I swerved over the line, and the driver shook his head. The trees overhead began to block out the stars.

"Your dad wrote that your mom's been in and out of Frank Wood Hospital in Phoenix, which is a mental hospital, and she may not be able to take care of you."

I didn't say anything. Mulligan brought his head back inside and tried to lean across my lap. I pushed him away.

"He said you were something special," said Jake. "Real smart. Said you skipped the third grade when you were younger."

"I did," I said.

"He said you had a garden back home. Used to raise vegetables."

"I did."

"He said you'd be some help at the ballpark."

"I think I have been."

"Yeah," said Jake, lighting up a cigarette. "You've been all right."

"He told me some things about you too," I said.

"He did, did he?"

"He did."

"Like what?"

"He said you'd drink all day if you could."

Jake blew smoke out the window and propped his foot up against the dashboard. "Not anymore, I wouldn't."

"He said you don't speak to your wife or kids anymore."

"Is that a fact?"

"You tell me," I said. "It's just something I heard."

Jake was quiet for a while. The sharp smell of pine drifted into the cab as we approached the driveway. Leaves and dust scattered across the road with the wind.

"Your dad was a harsh man," said Jake.

I nodded. "He could be."

"He never thought I was much help to him growing up."

"Well," I said. "What help were you?"

When we came up to the house I parked the truck next to the vegetable garden, long abandoned, the grass pushing over the soil. On the house, one of the gutters leaned crooked off the roof. I switched off the motor and sat still. Jake opened the door and let Mulligan out but didn't move from the cab. We could hear the crickets out in the woods.

"I don't know, Grady," Jake finally said. "I guess I was never good for much."

Jake didn't watch as much TV as he claimed, and some nights after we got back from the ballpark we'd sit in beach chairs on the second-story roof and looked at the stars. It was cold late in the evening and sometimes I'd throw a thick blanket over my legs. Jake sat next to me and dropped the ashes from his cigarettes into a can filled with topsoil. I learned that when you look straight up around midnight in late summer you can spot Vega, a blue-white star that shines bright in a cluster of other, duller stars in the constellation Lyra.

"Most constellations don't look anything like they're supposed to," said Jake. "Cassiopeia is supposed to be some lady sitting on a chair, but it looks more like the letter W, and Sagittarius is the archer, but he looks just like a teapot. See that orange star just south of Vega?"

"No."

"Right there," he said, pointing with the end of his cigarette. "Right below Vega. It's the beginning of Scorpio, which actually does look like you'd expect it to. That arc there is the claws of the scorpion and that hook of stars just underneath it is the tail."

"If you say so."

"I do."

"How do you know so much about this?" I said.

He leaned forward in the chair and glanced down into the yard. A pair of groundhogs stood near the edge of the woods, silhouetted in the light of the stars. One of them bent down and dug into the grass, his front paws working like shovels. We watched them in silence for a while, until Jake got caught up in a coughing fit and the groundhogs stood listening, still as tree stumps, and then meandered into the woods. We were up high enough to see over the treetops, and up on the horizon I could see Jupiter appear, the first planet Jake had pointed out to me the week before.

"How do you know so much about the sky?" I asked again.

"Me and my kids used to sit up here. They learned about it at some class they took at the community center."

"How old are your boys?"

"The oldest will be eighteen this year, and the younger one's a couple years older than you."

"Where do they live?"

"I'm not sure."

"Don't you ever call them?"

He took a drag off his cigarette. "There's not much point."

I picked up the binoculars and put them to my eyes. The moon that night was almost full, and it dimmed our view of a lot of the constellations. I squinted as I looked through the lenses, and then when my eyes began to adjust I could make out the giant crater on the south end of the moon, with the lunar Alps stretching out in gray and black. There was a strong breeze that night, the smell of burned wood drifting from the brush fire of one of Jake's neighbors.

"You must be proud of your little stunt tonight," I said.

"Oh," he said. "That's just part of the job."

"I bet," I said. "I bet that's not in the job description."

With two outs in the fourth inning, Gastonia finally got a man on base. When he took a lead off first, digging his heels into the baseline, he sank about an inch and a half into the dirt. He tried to steal second anyway and got nailed by the catcher with a few steps to spare. The runner walked back to first and swiped his foot at the line, kicking up enough peat moss to make the umpire have a closer look. The home crowd jeered at him. After a huddle with both managers, the umpire ordered the hole to be filled in, so Jake went out with the wheelbarrow, containing mostly the same mixture we'd put in the night before, and filled it over top. Because the baseline then had a mound of sand and muck sticking up on the line, the umpire had Jake water it down, so Jake looped the hose out onto the field and sprayed it over. It all resulted in a kind of overgrown swamp area near first base.

"I think I saw a few fish flopping around out there," I said.

Jake nodded. "We'll see if we can't catch us one or two tomorrow night."

The mailbox sat at the end of the gravel driveway, and every night when we returned from the ballpark Jake would walk down the road with Mulligan, returning a few minutes later, sticking his head into my room. "Nothing came," he would say.

"Okay."

My room had a banner for the Atlanta Braves and a chart of the stars on the ceiling that I began to study. A few clothes, about my size, hung on the rack in the closet—a red shirt with pineapple designs on the front, a black pair of corduroys, and two thick winter jackets with fur lining.

I placed my books on a shelf above one of the desks and slipped my clothes into the top drawer of the dresser. I didn't spend much time in the room because Jake and I were at the ballpark five, sometimes six days out of the week. We arrived at nine or so, after stopping at a diner on the highway for coffee and french toast. If there was a game that night, then we stayed at least until eleven o'clock, eating dinner from foil wrappers. I became pretty good at spotting sunken divots and soft spots in the outfield that we filled with dirt and soil, and the holes in the batter's box and pitcher's mound that we packed with clay.

During the games I could sit in the dugout with the team if I wanted to, but I didn't want to. The players were the kind of men who held spitting contests while the sides were changing, and they told dumb stories about high school—usually involving narrow escapes from the police and strange encounters with women from New York in the backseats of their cars. Mulligan sat in the stands with me, raising his ears at the sound of a ball struck hard or a child screaming in the family section near right field. Mostly, I just read during the games.

I found a lot of books about vegetable gardening in the town library. The soil in the foothills of North Carolina is good for a number of food crops, particularly potatoes and soybeans, and by the end of July

I'd pulled the weeds and overgrown grass out from the small garden at Jake's house. On our day or two off I began to plant a few rows of onions, carrots, and some other winter vegetables.

One day Jake walked out and stood over me as I knelt in the dirt. "What'd you do to my shovel?"

"What do you mean?"

He picked it up and fingered the blade. "You cut holes in it."

"I made a serrated edge so I could cut back the weeds. I didn't see a hoe anywhere."

"What'd you cut the holes with?"

"The file in your toolbox."

"Did you blunt it?"

I looked up at him. "Yes I blunted it, that's what it's there for."

"I was going to use that."

"I bet."

"What kind of seeds are those?" he said.

"Leek."

"What's that?"

"It's like an onion."

He stuck the shovel into the dirt. "Nothing's going to come up here. Winter's going to start in a few months."

"They'll be up about then."

"Nothing's grown here for a while," he said.

"That's because you haven't planted anything."

"You sure they're going to be up before winter?"

"No."

"Then why are you doing it?"

I stuck the trowel into the ground and scooped up the soil I'd put down the week before. I'd had to dig up the rocks and tree roots and just then was placing seeds in the ground.

"Because if nothing comes up this year, then something will come up next year. You've got to make the ground think like a garden."

"Where'd you learn that?"

"In a book," I said. "They're these thick things with words in them. I'll show you one sometime."

He just stood there, so after a while I put him to work digging five-inch-deep pockets along the left side of the garden. He stuck the shovel into the ground with his boot and chucked the dirt onto the grass.

"Could you keep that in a pile, please?" I said. "We'll need it to fill in the holes."

He didn't say anything, but he started scooping it into something resembling a pile.

"And could you try to keep them in a straight line?" I said.

"What's it matter if it's in a straight line?"

"It matters to me."

"So?"

"So," I said. "This is my garden. I'm in charge of it. You're in charge of the baseball field and I'm your assistant there. If you want to help out here, then you're my assistant."

"What are you paying?"

"Nothing," I said.

"Nothing?" he said. "What's the matter, you saving your money for something?"

I dropped seeds into the holes that he made and covered them up with dirt. I eyed the garden hose hanging on a nail on the side of the house. At the bottom of the hose were long holes, worn away over time.

"Grady?"

"Yeah?"

"You saving your money for something?"

"Maybe."

"Like what?"

"Nothing."

He shoveled another hole and flipped the dirt onto the growing pile. Looking up, he paused for a moment and said, "It's going to be a good night for watching the stars. Those clouds are moving out."

I packed the dirt flat on top of the seeds and then wondered why I'd done that. They needed loose soil so the plant could reach through. I stuck the trowel into the ground and turned it back and forth.

"If you say so," I said.

That Sunday night Jake took an old white sheet out from the closet and pinned it up over the fireplace in the den. From the basement he brought up a large, gray film projector and sat on the couch while he threaded a line of film into the feeder. Mulligan stretched out on his belly on the thick rug and kept an eye on the ice cream that I'd filled in two bowls. When Jake was finished, he flipped off the lights and turned the projector toward the wall. Backward letters and dark lines, like hair, shot across the screen, and then numbers counted down from seven to two.

Two shapes in the water, out of focus, splashed and kicked at each other until the camera moved closer, and I spotted the dark-haired head of my father as he waved to shore. The film was grainy and yellowed, and everything was in fast motion, like time itself moved faster back then. When they came out of the water, Jake was by far the taller of the two, broad-shouldered and wiry. He lay facedown on a picnic table and pretended to swim through the air, laughing like an idiot. My father stood a little ways behind him, wiping the water out of his ear with a towel, his body skinny enough that I could count his ribs and collarbones.

"That place was called Holden's Creek," said Jake, licking at the ice cream on his spoon. "It was about a half-mile away from the neighborhood we grew up in. Your dad was there all the time. He was a damn good swimmer."

"Who's behind the camera?"

"I don't know. Mom died when your father was about ten, and he looks older than that here."

"Was it your father?"

"No," said Jake. "It wouldn't have been him."

A dog trotted into the picture, a long-haired collie mix, and Jake picked it up by the front paws and began to dance. Behind them, the long leaves of a willow tree leaned forward with the breeze. My father sat on the picnic table, already pulling his shirt over his head and cleaning the dirt from between his toes. He glanced at Jake and the dog for a moment and then rolled his eyes.

"I bet your dad's about thirteen there. He moved away, you know, probably the next year. He lived in Seattle with our grandmother, our mom's mom, and then he went straight into the Coast Guard from there."

"What'd you do?"

"I just hung around home. They used to have a racetrack up near where we lived, and I always had the idea that I'd buy a stock car and get onto the circuit, but that never panned out."

"And then you got married?"

"No. I didn't get married for a while. I moved around a bit, taking a job here and there. I worked a lot of construction jobs. They were always easy to find in those days, probably still are. I met my wife in New Mexico of all places."

I looked at him. "My mom's from there."

"Is she?" he said. "I didn't know that. I never met your mom. But lots of good people come from around there."

"I'd like to see it one day," I said.

Jake set his bowl down on the floor for Mulligan. "You probably will. You've got your whole life ahead of you."

I shrugged. "If you say so."

"I do."

The film split to Jake and my dad in the backyard of a house, a wire fence standing crooked behind them. They both wore small, tight boxing gloves. Jake hopped from toe to toe, bare-chested, tapping my dad on the forehead and then leaping away. Dad kept his head low, sweat spots staining the arms of his T-shirt, stalking Jake slowly, not wasting punches until he was close enough. Jake talked to the camera, but there was no sound, and he stopped every once in a while to wind up his arm as if he was going to throw a wide hook, but Dad kept his gloves up and Jake backed off again.

By the middle of August the Knights had crept to within seven games of first place, but then they foundered on a weekend road trip and were eliminated from playoff contention. On our days off I worked at the weeds in the garden, sometimes at night under a full moon, and Jake brought home two buckets from the ballpark so we could water the vegetables in the evenings. The phone never rang in the house. I picked the receiver up from the cradle every few days or so, just to make sure the dial tone was still there.

During the late innings of games Jake sat in the stands with me and Mulligan, and if there was some kind of action down on the field, he'd point or nod his head at a base runner or an infielder.

"See that shortstop? He's checking the distance between him and second base because of the runner at first. And the third baseman, he's got to cover the gap. If that batter's any good, he can knock a line drive over the bag at third and score the runner."

In between innings I pointed out things in my books, like the picture of the mako shark. "Indigenous to southern climates only," I said.

Jake squinted and looked at the book. "You don't say."

"It does."

On the day before the final home stand, Jake had me cut the outfield extra low near the foul lines, hoping to turn some of the team's doubles into triples, and long after the sunset, he brought a shovel and a pail of dirt out to the pitcher's mound. He put his foot to the blade and dug out a concave shape into the front of the mound, where the pitcher's foot might land.

"What are you doing?" I asked.

He scooped the dirt into the wheelbarrow. "Scouting report on Burlington says they got this new kid. One hell of a fastball. Keeps it low and outside. The Knights can't hit low balls, never could."

"So?"

"So, when this kid goes into his windup, his foot's going to hit the dirt about a quarter second later than he thought it would, and that ball's going to float up over the plate like a giant piñata."

I stood with my hands in my pockets. "How many games do you think you've won for the Knights this year?"

He considered that. "About four or five. Not nearly enough."

I knelt and packed the dirt down with my hand, smoothing it over so it would be hard for the umpire to spot. Jake picked up a baseball and threw it into the outfield, and Mulligan jumped up from one of the on-deck circles and chased after it.

"What do you do in the off season, Jake?"

He shrugged. "I work a little in town at a hardware store that an old friend of mine owns, and I still come out to the field every once in a while. Make sure that nobody's messed with it. I'll be pretty busy all the way up to October, going to lay down some new sod in the outfield this autumn, before it gets too cold."

"Sounds like a lot of work."

"Probably will be," he said.

I looked up at him. "I'll probably be gone in a few days," I said. "I'm sorry I won't be around to help you."

He looked at me. "Is that a fact? You hear something from your mom?"

"No. But she'll be ready to take me by the end of the month."

"How do you figure?"

I looked out at the highway past the stadium. A tractor trailer made its way up the hill, and smaller cars passed it on the outside. "It's just what we'd talked about," I said.

"When did you talk to her?"

"Before I came out here."

"Oh," he said. He put the shovel over his shoulder. "I don't remember you mentioning that."

"Maybe I didn't."

"Is she going to send for you?"

"Doesn't matter," I said. "I've almost got enough money to get a train ride there."

"I see." He placed the rest of the tools into the wheelbarrow. "How much you short?"

"About thirty dollars."

He picked up the wheelbarrow and began to walk toward the shed. "I bet you I can spot you that if you're still short."

I followed behind him. "I'll pay you back."

"No. We'll just call it an end-of-the-season bonus."

"If you say so."

"I do."

We put the tools away in the shed and snapped the lock shut. The truck was parked outside in the space closest to the gate. Jake said he'd drive that night, so I opened the passenger door for Mulligan and then climbed in. Up in the sky, the moon was absent, and I could spot Vega just to the north of center, bright as I'd seen it. We pulled out onto the highway.

"Arizona's a good place," said Jake. "I'll miss having you around, though. You've been a lot of help to me."

"I'll write you a letter when I get there."

"Do that."

I played with a strip of fabric hanging off the seat cover. "Are you going to write me back?"

"I suppose so."

"I'd like to hear how the garden turns out," I said. I rolled up the window. "Are you going to keep working at it?"

"If you want me to."

"I do."

"All right then," he said.

The road was empty on the ride back. We didn't pass a single car on the state highway or the narrow road leading to the house. When we pulled onto the driveway, the trees covered up the stars and the headlights glowed, shining on the leaves and the tree branches fallen to the ground.

"Thanks for showing me the stars," I said. "I learned a lot while I was here."

"Glad to hear it."

"I'll probably show my mom some of them."

"I'm sure she'd like that," Jake said. He began to roll up his window. "Tell you what. You remember which one Scorpio was?"

"Yep."

"And what's its main star?"

"Antares."

"Okay," he said. "Scorpio's going to rise in the sky as autumn comes, and on into winter. You try to check out Antares every once in a while. Around midnight or so, and I'll try and look at it the same time here."

I considered that. I looked over at him. He wasn't factoring in the two-hour time difference. I thought about saying something smart. "That sounds good," I said.

"All right then."

When we came out from the tree line, we could see two small shadows stand up in the dark, like rocks suddenly come to life. As we approached, one of them began to lope toward the woods. The second groundhog paused and then chased after the first. I opened the truck door and Mulligan tore out across the yard after them. I watched him run, but the groundhogs made the edge of the trees before he was halfway there.

It looked like someone had dropped a grenade in the garden patch. Half-eaten onions lay scattered across the soil, and a short trench, where the carrots had been planted, stretched in shadows in the dirt. Roots from the leek plants were tangled around the makeshift wooden stands, snapped in two. We could hear Mulligan's barking from down the driveway, and the scent of the loose earth hovered above the wreckage, sweet and sharp.

Jake stood beside the truck as I poked at the some of the carrots, bits and pieces missing, and their long, stringy roots wrapped in knots.

"That's a lot of hard work ruined," he said.

I nodded but didn't say anything.

He walked up the driveway after Mulligan and left me kneeling in the soil. I picked up a string of carrots, half-grown, and wiped at them. In the shed I switched the light on and found the trowel and the shovel, slinging them over my shoulder with the two empty buckets. I returned a few minutes later and dragged a heavy bag of fresh soil down the path. With the moon gone it was dark in the patch, but some of the brighter stars were beginning to appear on the horizon. Jake's boots crunched in the gravel down near the woods. I knelt in the soil and began to separate the vegetables, making two piles in the corners.

Fixing torn-up divots in the outfield at the baseball stadium was good practice for the job. I was already making calculations in my head—the number of seeds I still had in the house, how much time I had before winter, which rows, as a whole, might be replanted, and where I might get some wire fencing to put up around the garden.

Jake walked up to the patch, and Mulligan trotted behind him, his head hanging low, defeated. Jake stood with one hand in his pocket, the other holding an envelope facedown. "Grady," he said.

I went back to separating the vegetables. "What's that?"

"It's for you."

I took the letter from him, smearing soil across the envelope. The return address was from Frank Wood Hospital, Arizona, but it was addressed to Jake, not me.

"It's for you," I said, handing it back.

"But it's about you."

"Take it."

He frowned but closed his fingers around it, pausing and then tearing the paper up the side. He slipped a letter out and unfolded it. Turning in place, he tried to catch some of the light from the stars, and I could see his eyes squinting and trying to focus. I thought I could hear those groundhogs out in the woods. I listened for them. Jake stood a few moments and I waited on him. He handed the letter back to me.

"My eyes aren't good enough," he said.

I took it from him and read it, pausing between words, trying to make out sentences in the starlight. Mulligan sniffed at the onions in the garden, and Jake lit up a cigarette, the first spark of tobacco mixing with the scent of the soil.

After a time, I folded the letter up and stuck it in my pocket. I picked up the trowel and began scooping dirt back into the short trench.

"Go through that pile," I said, motioning to the rest of the vegetables. "Pick out anything worth saving."

I knelt in the dirt and dug new holes in the earth. Jake brought pails of water from inside the house and a stack of wood from behind the shed. He set the lengths of wood one by one on a bigger log, splitting them in thirds down the side with a hatchet. With the hammer from the truck cab, he pounded the fresh stakes around the edge of the garden, making a wall a foot and a half high. On the corners he put longer stakes, like the towers of a frontier fort. While I replanted the carrots and onions, dropping seeds into fresh holes, Jake disappeared inside and returned later with an armful of wire hangers. He clipped them near the top with wire cutters, twisted them together, and ran them like string from the four corners of the fence.

We worked all night, stopping only to share coffee from a thermos. When the orange glow from the sun appeared over the mountains, I had to squint from the brightness. All night long we'd worked in the light from stars.

I remembered then something my mom had told me. The first star at night appears like a point on a map—the only point—and from that position, other stars emerge. They scatter in unpredictable places, depending on where you are, and they begin to create meaningful constellations. When the sky becomes full, in the middle hours of the night, it's easy to pick out the dominant star—Vega on some nights, Polaris on others. But it's difficult to remember, looking up at the map, which star came first, which is the one that holds the rest in place. You think to yourself: which one of those stars up there was the brightest, when it mattered the most?

THE PROBLEM
WITH FLIGHT

Grimsley kept a flower stem in his pocket, not so much for good luck, but to keep bad luck away, a trick his mother had taught him. In the summertime, he never wore a hat after dark. Of these things, he was sure. An apple or a tomato without a bruise was bad luck, as was reading the obituaries, unless you knew someone in there. Bats brought good luck, but you didn't want too many of them. A candle reflected in glass was a good sign, but its reflection in a mirror was, if possible, to be avoided. He never let a younger person take his picture. A moon in the morning brought great luck, and snow and sunshine on the same day was even better. Hail, though, was trouble all around.

In the office of the lumberyard he put on his galoshes, his hat (it was winter), and his overcoat and limped out into the moonlight, into the sleet and snow. In the yard he checked the fence line for breaks and shined his flashlight under the stacks of oak wood in the main yard. The machine saws were unplugged, and there were no teenagers hiding there: it was the wrong season for pranks. At the shoreline Grimsley splashed salt water on his face, watched the ripple of stars in the waves of the bay. Inside the mill, he dropped a bit of sand into his shoe for luck and rubbed mentholatum on his knee because it was old and it hurt. He kept away from the coffee on his doctor's orders. He warmed himself at the woodstove and watched the slow hands of the time clock and waited for his shift to end.

On his drive home he passed the lines of pickups and station wagons, lights on, driving toward work and school, slow in the morning's slush and ice. He watched for animals from the woods. They came out fast if you didn't keep an eye out. Killing a raccoon was bad luck, and deer was worse.

At home, he left his boots just inside the trailer door, and he changed his socks because that was good for his circulation. His wife was in the kitchen, and an omelet—spinach, which he didn't much like—was frying in a pan. Mona rubbed lotion on her arm—an old habit, she'd been burned bad as a child—and squinted up at him as he sat down. She looked tired and old, although she was ten years younger than him.

"You put your glasses on, you could see," he said.

"They hurt my eyes this early."

"I could be a serial murderer with a chain saw, for all you could tell."

"I know your walk," Mona said. "A man with a chain saw doesn't come in here with just his socks on."

He took a seat. "You get that prescription changed and you'd be all right."

"I had it changed, and the lenses were too heavy. I'm not having that same fool conversation with you this morning. I can smell a cigarette on your clothes. You got no business giving me any lectures."

Grimsley decided not to argue with her. It was bad luck. Although his mother hadn't taught him that, he'd learned it on his own. Mona set the lotion aside, pushed her chair away from the table. At the stove she flipped the omelet, pushed down with the spoon. They listened to the sizzle of grease, the ice slipping from the trailer outside. The sun was beginning to rise. He switched the lamp off and watched the shadows of trees on the frozen pond, the birds pecking at the snow. Mona set the omelet on a plate, brought him a knife and fork, a mug of juice. He ate quickly: the spinach didn't taste so bad when it burned his tongue.

"Today's Thursday," Mona said.

Grimsley concentrated on the omelet. He counted the bites remaining—six if he was lucky—and said nothing.

"You said you'd go over there by the end of the week," she said.

"Saturday's the end of the week."

"Saturday you'll be out on your boat, and tomorrow you'll tell me a man needs to enjoy his Friday. Today's a good day to go."

"Is she going to the hospital today?"

Mona sat down in the chair across from him. "The next time that woman goes'll be the last time, and then you'll have that hanging on your head. Don't make me get mean with you."

Grimsley thought she was being mean already, but he kept the thought to himself. He ate a bite of omelet. He didn't like visiting the dying—that was big-time bad luck unless you were family or a minister—and he didn't like making promises without first thinking them through. He looked over at his wife.

"I'm just fixing things, right?"

"The woman's granddaughter is staying with her, and she could certainly use a little help. There's a hole in the bathroom and a leak in the kitchen. How'd you like some water running through your kitchen this time of year?"

"I guess I wouldn't like it very much."

"You're pushing it," she said.

He looked at his watch, bought a little time while he thought things through.

"I'll go over in the afternoon," he said.

"This afternoon?"

"By the time you come home, I'll be there and back."

"And those things'll be fixed?"

"If I can fix them in an afternoon, they'll be fixed. If not, tomorrow."

"On a Friday?"

"Nothing like helping people on a Friday."

Mona picked up the bottle of lotion and put her glasses on. "Helping someone doesn't have a time limit."

Shelby set her book on the dresser and picked up the oxygen line from the tank. Her grandmother pressed her head back against the pillows, squinted her eyes. She coughed up something gray and solid into her mask. Shelby wiped it out with a handkerchief. She rubbed her grandmother's temples, something the woman had liked weeks before, although now Shelby couldn't be sure. She cut back on the oxygen, set her grandmother up against the pillows, brushed the hair out of the woman's eyes. Out the window, she could see the shadows of trees against the pond and a single bird, pecking at the snow. Later, the visiting nurse—Karl, a man Shelby had a secret crush on, was terrified at the thought—changed the woman's dressings, the bedsheets, gave the woman an injection of pain relief though a tube into her leg. Shelby read her books in the bedroom, and when her grandmother slept, in the kitchen. History mostly, things she liked: Roman emperors who built a seawall for fishermen, who supported the arts and theater, who poisoned their fathers (she didn't like that), who built roads through what would become France.

Over the past weeks, she'd read about cave dwellings, about sea scrolls, about Amelia Earhart (two books about her), and about one of the first known cartographers, a Russian named Yirvus. She walked to the library in town on Mondays, a nurse—not Karl—stayed for most of that day, and Shelby brought back as many books as would fit in her pack. Her grandmother had been dying for many weeks now. Shelby had dropped out of the tenth grade. She read about da Vinci, about James Farmer, and about the first woman to reach the North Pole. She read and reread a book on the Dust Bowl of 1934. Shelby kept a notebook, copied passages that she wanted to remember. She'd not been much of a reader before, had liked television and the radio, but the sound bothered her grandmother.

In her reading, Shelby found that she didn't much like the British, though that was likely due to Churchill. She did like a nun in the sixteenth century named Elizabeth Byrd who had done little of anything, but who seemed to notice a lot: waterbirds, the sky at night, dragonflies. Meriwether Lewis was the best writer, Shelby thought, although Wilbur Wright was close behind. She read at a varied pace—mostly depending on her grandmother.

On this morning, she took out her pen, opened her notebook. *Do you not insist too strongly on the single point of mental ability? To me, it seems that a thousand other factors, each rather insignificant in itself, in the aggregate influenced the event ten times more than mere mental ability or inventiveness. If the wheels of time could be turned back, it is not at all probable that we would do again what we have done. . . . It was due to a peculiar set of circumstances which might never occur again.*

She read for a half hour, copying a passage here and there. After, she checked on her grandmother again, turned the heat up in the room, placed two tablets on the woman's tongue, sitting her up straight, pressing a cup of water to the lips. The woman looked at her but her eyes didn't seem to focus. When she was set against the pillows again, she mumbled, "It's too deep out there. You need to come in a little."

Shelby sat on the nightstand and brushed the woman's hair, held her hand for a few minutes. A man's voice from the other room opened her eyes. She placed her grandmother's arm back under the covers and switched off the lamp. She closed the door behind her.

"Good morning," said the man. He stood in the doorway to the trailer. He was old and stooped a little, seemed to keep the weight off one leg.

"Yes sir," said Shelby.

He paused for a moment, as if she'd addressed someone else.

"I'm here to fix some things," he said. "My wife's name is Mona, and I believe she talked with you."

"All right."

She showed him the pipes in the kitchen, the aluminum pan filled with water and the towels spread on the floor. It was cold in the trailer, a draft seemed to come from the bathroom. He bent and took the flashlight from his pocket, inspected things, ran his finger along the rust and the mold.

"That's behind the wall," he said. "You had anyone look at this?"

"No."

"Why not?"

"Don't have a lot of money."

Grimsley looked at the wall under the sink again. "That won't cost much."

She showed him the bathroom and the plank of wood on the roof. The bulb over the sink flickered. He brought a chair from the kitchen, set it in the tub, had her hold it still. He stepped up, pulled away some plaster, pressed the wood back, inspected the hole. A bit of snow fell down in his eye. He felt the damp along the ceiling.

"This whole thing is rotten," he said.

"How much do you think?"

He looked at her, genuinely confused. "How much do I think?"

"How much do you think it will all cost?"

The light flickered in the bathroom again. Grimsley looked up.

"That do that much?"

"All the time," she said.

"Anywhere else?"

"All over."

He looked down at her and smiled a little. "You're having all kinds of trouble."

Her expression didn't change.

Grimsley paused. There was something off about the girl, he thought. He stepped down from the chair. He felt a sting in his knee, almost slipped when he took his weight off it, caught himself with his hand on the tub.

"You all right?" Shelby said.

He closed the lid on the toilet, sat down. He pushed his fingers to the base of his kneecap.

"This thing acts up on me when it's got a mind to."

He sat for a while, rubbing at the knee. The pain was sharp, behind the cap. He watched the lamp bulb flicker, let the pain run its course. After, he limped into the kitchen, sat down on the remaining chair.

"Do you have some ice?" he said.

"I have some snow outside."

He nodded. "That'll do."

She found a plastic bag and went out. Grimsley rolled up his pant leg, looked at the blue skin. He took the bag from her when she returned, stretched his leg, and set the pack on his knee.

"It'll be about fifty for the roof," he said. "We might skip the plaster, just put some insulation up there with some plastic. The wiring might be extra."

"I think the wires will have to wait."

"It's bad luck to let things go."

"Maybe so," she said. "My name's Shelby. I can get half that fifty now, and maybe the other half in a week or two."

"That'll do. People call me Grimsley."

"Mr. Grimsley, when'll your man come?"

Grimsley looked up from his knee. "What man?"

"The man who's going to fix the roof."

"I'm going to fix it."

Shelby looked at his knee. "I can't help you if you take a fall."

He looked back at her. "You're not going to help me if I take a fall?"

"I'll help you," she said. "But I can't pay for the doctor or anything."

"I got enough doctors already."

"One of the nurses might be around," the girl said. "They could have a look at you."

He frowned. "You're talking like I'm already out there with a broken neck."

"I'm just saying," she said. She tapped her knuckles three times against the wooden table. "I hope nothing happens."

"Don't knock on wood," said Grimsley. "Snap your fingers instead, it works better."

When his knee felt better, he hobbled back to his trailer across the snow. He found his toolbox and some old work clothes. For some reason, the girl, Shelby, reminded him of his own sister, a woman he owed a few phone calls to. He hadn't spoken with his sister since last Christmas. She lived on the other side of the country now. There was always something about her that made Grimsley feel inadequate and foolish. Like he thought their conversations were about one thing, and then they turned out to be about something else—something over his head. The girl made him feel that way. As if she was having two conversations, one with him and the other with someone more interesting and important.

He drove into town and found the pipes he'd need. He bought some washers, a large roll of plastic, a collection of nails and screws, and a pack of cigarettes that he hid under the maps in his glove compartment. He drove to the sawmill and picked out some pieces of scrap wood, borrowed a ladder from the foreman. In the old woman's trailer, he turned off the water and set the plastic down in front of the sink, turned the faucet until it ran dry. He didn't much like the smell in the trailer—mold and dust, and another smell that came from the woman's bedroom that he tried not to think about. Shelby sat at the kitchen table, had put on an extra sweater, watched him as he bent in front of the sink, as he set himself flat on his back. She took out her pen and the Wright brothers book, and she went back to her journal.

It is my belief that flight is possible, and, while I am taking up the investigation for pleasure rather than profit, I think there is slight possibility of achieving fame and fortune from it. It is almost the only great problem which has not been pursued by a multitude of investigators, and therefore carried to a point where further progress is very difficult. I am certain I can reach a point much in advance of any previous workers in the field even if complete success is not attained just at present. At any rate, I shall have an outing of several weeks and see a part of the world I have never before visited.

Grimsley tried to be quiet with the wrench against the pipes, not for Shelby but for the woman. He pulled out the backboard, wiped up the water in the back, set the rusted pipes on the plastic.

"You want some help?" said Shelby.

He looked at her. He almost said, You can help by leaving me alone, but that would've been big-time bad luck.

"I'm all right," he said instead.

"I could hold the flashlight."

He sighed, he hoped silently. "If you want."

She set her notebook aside and sat on the floor next to him. When he asked, she passed him a metal file, some sandpaper, a plastic washer. They could hear the ping of rain on the rooftop of the trailer.

"That'll get in the bathroom," he said.

"I put the wood back."

He held up his left arm, looked at his watch. She shined the flashlight there.

"Not sure we'll get to that today," he said.

"That's all right."

"Don't you go to school or something?"

"I dropped out."

He was surprised. "Really?"

"The studying gives me problems."

"Maybe you studied too much," he said.

"Never heard of that."

"Too much of something is bad luck."

"How do you know when it's too much?"

He looked back at her through a crook in the pipes. "The studying?"

"Anything."

Grimsley considered her question. He set the wrench against the floor. This was exactly the type of conversation he'd been worrying about. "I don't think it's my business to tell you to go back to school or not," he said.

She blinked. "I didn't know I'd asked you that."

"Isn't that what I just said?"

"Sort of," she said. "But I didn't know you were thinking that."

He frowned. "You see that scrap of sandpaper?"

She found it under his boot, and he took it from her, handed back the wrench. He worked the grit off the edge of a pipe, closed his eyes so as not to get blinded by the falling sand.

"How old are you?" she said.

"It'd be bad luck to tell you," said Grimsley

"You look kind of old, but you act a lot younger."

He took up the wrench and readjusted the flashlight in her hands. If he just kept his mouth shut here, he was going to be in for all kinds of good luck.

"Did you finish school?" said the girl.

The question seemed to indicate that he hadn't, though that was not her tone.

"Are you asking if I graduated?"

"Yes."

"I graduated, but I didn't end up walking in the ceremony."

"That's strange," she said. "Why not?"

He didn't answer that. He had been in jail at the time. He'd driven drunk and killed two of his friends who were riding with him. The memory came back sharp and clear. He suddenly wanted to get out from under the sink and away from this girl.

"Are you glad you finished school?" Shelby said.

"I hadn't really ever thought of it," said Grimsley.

The girl thought that over. "That doesn't push me either way."

At home, Grimsley set his flashlight back on the dresser, put the toolbox away in the closet. He changed his socks, which made him feel better. In the kitchen, he sliced up onions and potatoes, took out the cream from the fridge, made some soup at the stove and left it to warm for Mona. He cut a few slices of bread and set them on his bowl and ate his dinner in front of the television, watching a game show and a special about penguins, who he thought were pretty stupid. He drank a beer so he could sleep, and as he set the empty bottle next to the empty bowl, he closed his eyes and propped his feet on the stool he'd carved when he was younger. He had a dream where he lay flat in the middle of a pond as snow fell on him, covering him until he looked like a large, irregular mountain range or a white sand dune. He was both under the snow and watching himself on TV. There were penguins under the ice who kept knocking, waking him up. The penguins were very adamant, as if he owed them something and they had arrived to collect. The snow felt hot, not cold, and it burned his skin. There was a narrator on TV who told him the man under the snow had been there a thousand years and would be there a thousand more.

When he woke, he could hear Mona in the kitchen, and he didn't know how long he'd been asleep. The TV was turned off, but he could see the blue glow of another set, out the window and in his neighbor's trailer. Mona brought her soup in from the kitchen and sat down next to him. She worked at a printer's shop all day, and the tips of her fingers were stained blue and red.

"How'd you do?" he said.

"Same as always. How'd you do?"

"That girl is frightening," he said. "She's like something out of one of those movies where people get possessed."

Mona looked at him. "You're definitely losing your mind. She seems like any other girl to me."

"You don't know things like I know," he said.

"And I'm grateful for it," said Mona.

She ate her soup, and he closed his eyes again. She'd wake him in another hour. The things he knew—or thought he knew—she'd begun to catalog in her mind. She thought she might like to remember them, if he went before her. She'd written some of them down on a paper bag she kept under her sweaters in the closet.

If a relative is sick, leave a lock of your hair outside your window, or, if you don't like them, a penny, face-up. Don't drop an unused line in the water: you're just asking for trouble. Some of his ideas made some sense to her: never kill a mud-dauber or a spider, and don't touch a dog's bone. Some of them, she didn't know what to make of: a fish with one eye should be thrown back in the water. Always stir a pot with a spoon, never a fork. And then she had her favorites: never wrestle a bear, no matter how much money you're offered. Don't make a wish on a shooting star. Make a promise instead, and keep it. And don't lie to your wife.

She dipped her spoon into the potato soup and watched her husband sleep.

In the morning, before the nurse arrived, Shelby called the doctor. Her grandmother slept quietly, but her arms and hands had turned a shade of blue. The doctor told her to put the oxygen away—it was no longer a relief to the woman and she would be more comfortable without the mask. There were only a few more days, he seemed sure this time, and after she'd changed her grandmother's nightgown, placed the tablets on her tongue, brushed the woman's hair and rubbed her hands and arms, Shelby took a page from her notebook, sat at the kitchen table, and wrote to her uncle in Chicago. When Karl arrived, she helped him with the bedsheets, with the sponge bath. She watched the man's fingers, which she'd always liked, and said little.

It was an odd thing, waiting for someone to die. Shelby had been passed from home to home throughout her life. This was her third stay with her grandmother, and she loved the woman, though she felt detached from her, as she often did from the world. Shelby wondered if there was a trick in her mind that she could learn, to connect again and hold a full heart. She had been very close with her grandfather. When she thought of her heart now, she thought it around a quarter full. She wondered if it was filling or falling.

Outside, the sun had appeared in a cloudless sky, although it was still quite cold. The ice on the pond glistened in yellow specks, and she watched a young boy—about her age—shoveling the steps to a trailer. Shelby waited for Grimsley after Karl left, took out her notebook at the table, brewed some coffee on the stove. She opened the dog-eared text. This time it was a quote from Orville Wright.

The sunsets here are the prettiest I have ever seen. The clouds light up in all colors in the background, with deep blue clouds of various shapes fringed with gold before. The moon rises in much the same style, and lights up this pile of sand almost like day. I have read my watch . . . on moonless nights without the aid of any light other than that of the stars shining on the canvas of the tent.

Grimsley set the ladder against the trailer, packed snow around the feet. He took the tool belt from his shoulder, hitched it around his waist. He slung the plastic tarp over his shoulder and made his way up the ladder. On the roof, he tested one foot, then the other, brushed off the snow, and removed the wood. A girl's face looked up at him through the hole.

"Hi," said Shelby.

He hadn't remembered seeing her smile before. It both relieved and further frightened him.

"Okay," said Grimsley.

"I got your money. Half of it, at least."

"All right," he said. "I'm supposed to not take it. I was told this morning."

She appeared to think that over. "On the one hand, I wish you'd take it. On the other hand, you should probably listen to your wife."

"Either way I'm screwed," he said.

He took some measurements on the roof, set the tarp over the hole, made his way back down the ladder. Inside, he noticed the bedroom door open a crack. He could see the old woman in the bed, the bottles and the tubes on the nightstand. He closed the door shut.

"We'll make some noise today," he said.

"She's beyond that now."

He took a cup of coffee although he didn't really want one. He placed the stopper in the bathtub drain. He set the chair back in the tub and took out his hammer. Stepping up, he took his balance, caught the plaster with the hook and pulled down. It came out easily, soaked through. He dropped what he took down into the tub, and Shelby handed him a pick and a chisel when he needed them. In a half hour he was covered in white dust, and the plaster from one wall to the other had been removed. He started in on the wood.

"You make your living doing this?" said Shelby.

"Pulling out plaster?"

"No. Doing handywork."

"Used to. Long time ago. I used to work the fish lines in Alaska. That was in the Stone Age. I work nights at the lumberyard now. Make sure nobody messes with the place."

"Do you like it?"

Grimsley hooked into a nail. "It's bad luck to complain about your job."

"Is it good luck to say you like it?"

"I guess."

"Well?"

Grimsley said nothing to that.

He pulled out bad wood for the next hour. Took a break and had another cup of coffee in the kitchen. Shelby disappeared into the bedroom, and again Grimsley smelled something he didn't like as she closed the door. His knee hurt, but it felt good compared with his shoulders. He wished he'd brought his cigarettes. While he waited, he looked at the girl's books—something about the wall in China and one about the Wright brothers. Another slim text was titled *Guadalcanal*. He opened her notebook, looked at her handwriting, and then closed it again. He'd pay for that one. That was super bad luck. He walked into the den and looked at some pictures. There were a lot of the grandmother with other people, although she didn't look much like the person he'd seen through the bedroom door.

There was one of Shelby, no frame, from what seemed to be a few years back. He picked it up and looked on the other side. It read, "sixth grade." He turned it back over and looked at her. The photo was of the school yearbook variety. Her smile seemed forced, although he didn't know what he could conclude from that observation. His sister came back to him then. He really should give her a call. She was only a few years younger than him and could be dead for all he knew. Beyond the pictures and the furniture, the trailer seemed sparse and empty.

He found that if he kept the girl busy, she didn't ask as many personal questions. They walked back to his and Mona's trailer in the snow, found the sawhorses under the steps, set them over their shoulders for the walk back. Grimsley measured out the scrap wood with the tape, set the boards across the horses. He showed Shelby how to cut with the electric saw, how to set her feet, how to cut in a straight line, not at an angle. Woodchips collected in the snow.

Inside, he set the beams in the tub, dropped a collection of nails in the soap rack. He measured and remeasured the ceiling, set the boards in the right order. Shelby stood next to him in the tub, holding the support beams across, although there wasn't much room for the both of them. It was all he could do to not whack one of their heads with the hammer, and their work slowed to a crawl.

It was Shelby's idea to climb up to the roof and stick her arm through the hole, keeping the beams in place and giving Grimsley more room. He set her fingers—she couldn't look in—and told her not to move them. As he hammered, he told her where to sit, where to move to, so the nails wouldn't stick her if they came out the roof. They worked from the left side across, and then from the right to the hole. As they neared the end, only Shelby's hand and wrist could be seen.

"Didn't think you'd come back."

At first, Grimsley thought Shelby had said it, but then he realized the voice had come from behind him. He turned on the chair, trying to keep his feet. The old woman stood in the doorway. Her nightgown had slipped off one of her shoulders, and her yellow teeth, a few of them missing, were clenched tight. She held a plastic hanger above her head like a club.

"Where's my sewing machine?" she said.

"I don't think it's in the bathroom," said Grimsley. He felt exposed, up on the chair. On the rooftop, he could hear Shelby begin to scramble down.

"Ronald will settle this between us," the woman said. "He'll be here in a minute."

Grimsley watched the hanger in the woman's hand. She looked frail and weak, but not above using it. He wished he were off the chair. He had a vision of broken hips.

"I don't know any Ronald," he said.

"You'll know him soon enough," said the woman.

"I don't doubt that."

"As soon as he gets here, you're going to be sorry."

He started to get down off the chair. "I'm already sorry," he said.

She held the hanger out in front of her. "You stay where you are, or I'll blow a hole clean through you."

Grimsley stopped moving. He stayed on the chair. "You got the wrong man."

"And you've got the wrong luck," she said.

He didn't like that at all.

Shelby appeared in the hallway, placed her arm across her grandmother's shoulders, but the woman took little notice. Grimsley didn't move. The girl whispered to the woman, words Grimsley could not make out. He looked down at the hammer in his hand, realized he had it gripped tight.

He stood there for another minute or two as Shelby talked to the woman. She didn't take her eyes off him, though. She didn't look at all like the woman in the pictures, not like the woman in the bed, either. If she'd had a gun, Grimsley bet she'd already have used it. Eventually, she handed the hanger back to Shelby.

As she turned back toward the bedroom, she looked at him once more. "You and I aren't through yet," she said.

The bedroom door closed behind them, and Grimsley stepped down off the chair. He collected his tools and left the wood in the tub. There was that smell in the hallway, stronger this time. Outside, he climbed up the ladder, tried to be as quiet as he could. Through the hole, he could see that only three planks remained, but he pulled the tarp over the gap, set the wood over the top.

When he climbed down the ladder, he took one of the sawhorses back to his trailer, stored it under the steps. He thought about not going back. He snapped his fingers a few times, and that made him feel better. When he returned, he waited for Shelby a few minutes, watched the ice out on the pond—dark in the center, thick and white near the edges. He wondered if there were penguins under there. A pile of leaves whirled with the wind. Grimsley pulled his collar up to his neck, checked his watch. He picked up the other sawhorse and headed home.

Shelby sat with her grandmother for most of that night. She watched the moon through the window, watched it disappear past the frame. She rubbed the woman's palms, the tips of her fingers. The woman didn't move much, although every hour or so her eyes opened—she was drugged up again—and she seemed to watch the end of her own nose. The woman's arms were now blue. In the morning, Shelby would call the doctor. The girl tried to eat a sandwich in the kitchen, had trouble keeping it down. She drank some apple juice and then some coffee.

Taking the chair from the tub, she set it next to her grandmother's bed, in the glow of the lamplight. She tried to read her Wright brothers book, scanned the same pages for an hour. Eventually, she turned to the middle, studied the dimensions of the brothers' glider: the warped wings, the elevated rudder. When she took her grandmother's hand, it felt cold, and Shelby found her wool cap and set it over the woman's head. The eyes were closed.

Shelby found if she whispered the words, she could make progress with the chapter about the first flight. She'd read for ten minutes, flip back to the pictures in the middle of the book. She studied a corner of the glider, then the other corner, thought of the machine as a series of lines. The faces of the fishermen, of the two brothers, of their sister seemed pale, ashen in the dim lamplight. Shelby dog-eared a picture of a derby hat, abandoned at the top of a dune. She read some more, took out her flashlight, set it at the top of the book, shined the light down.

Shelby found a passage she'd always liked. Her grandmother's eyes were closed, but she read to her.

I have asked dozens of bicycle riders how they turn to the left. I have yet to find a single person who stated the facts correctly when first asked. They almost invariably said that to turn to the left, they turned the handlebar to the left and as a result made a turn to the left. But on further questioning them, some would agree that they first turned the handlebar a little to the right, and then as the machine inclined to the left, they turned the handlebar to the left and as a result made the circle, inclining inwardly.

Shelby took her grandmother's hand. It felt colder still.

"He's a smart bear," said the woman.

In the morning, Grimsley slept late. It was his first of two days off. He hadn't told Mona about the woman. "We're almost there," he'd said. "Be done today." She made some breakfast: egg whites (she did that once a week) and grits (which he didn't like). He cleaned his plate. Afterward, they watched cartoons on the TV, and Mona wrote cards to her family and rubbed lotion into her arm during commercials. There were more penguins in the cartoons, and it annoyed Grimsley again. At noon, he looked for his toolbox in the closet where it wasn't, and found it under the bed where it was. He changed into work clothes. Outside, he couldn't find any sand, so he dropped some snow into his shoe, which soaked through his sock and made his steps squeak as he walked through the maze of homes.

In the distance, Grimsley could see an ambulance parked along the road, lights off, and the door to the woman's trailer was open. There was movement through the window. He thought for a few moments about turning around, but he made it to the steps and set his toolbox in the snow. The ladder had fallen during the night. It lay sideways, pointing out toward the pond. He could see a man dressed in white through the doorway. The man held the end of a stretcher. A pair of feet were wrapped in a blanket. Grimsley walked around in the yard, kicking at the snow, digging a short trench near the side of the house.

When they brought her out, the blanket was over the woman's face. Shelby stood in the doorway. The men took the stretcher into the ambulance, and one of them came back and talked with Shelby for a minute. He handed her a clipboard, and she signed a few papers.

After that she went and stood near Grimsley. He put his hands in his pockets and didn't say anything. They watched the ambulance as it pulled out of the yard and passed through the mud and the snow. A few heads—eyes and chins—watched from windows. The land was flat there, and they could see the ambulance for a few miles as it headed north toward the highway. It disappeared in a stretch of trees and then reappeared in the clearing beyond. Eventually, the ambulance went below a hill and didn't come back up.

"I'm sorry," Grimsley said.

"It was coming."

Grimsley looked at his toolbox. "How're you doing?"

"I'm all right."

"That's good." He thought about going to get Mona.

"Can you finish the job today?"

Grimsley shrugged. He wanted to say something else. "Just an hour or two."

"I'm going to be packing up," she said. "So if you could do it on your own, that'd be best."

"All right."

Shelby went inside, and Grimsley picked up his toolbox and followed her. In the bathroom he set the planks back in the tub and took out his measuring line. When he went to get the chair, Shelby was setting the pictures in stacks on the couch. Some dishes and glasses were already in boxes on the floor.

"I could get you some more boxes at the yard," he said.

"I've had them for a while," she said. "Been keeping them in the closet."

"Oh," he said.

He took the chair into the bathroom and set it in the tub, placed the hammer and nails in the sink. Then he came back out.

"Where are you going to stay?"

The girl looked up from the boxes. "I'm headed out to Bremerton. It's near Seattle. One of my sisters lives there. Bus leaves on Tuesday."

"That's good."

"Yep."

Grimsley went back to the bathroom and picked up the hammer. He climbed up on the chair and set one of the planks against the ceiling. He stuck in a nail and hammered it through. He hammered a few more, and the taps echoed in the bathroom, out to the hallway. When the plank was in place, he climbed down and went back to the den.

"You need a ride on Tuesday?"

"You offering one?"

"Yep."

"I've got to be there at eight," she said.

"I'm up early."

"All right," she said.

Grimsley went back and finished putting up the rest of the planks. The hole in the roof disappeared as he slipped the smallest board into the last gap. He took it back out, filed the edges to make it fit. He heard something small fall in the den.

"You all right?" he called.

"Yep."

He hammered the board into place, put his hammer away in the toolbox. Picking up the caulking gun, he snipped the edge off with his knife. After, he went back to the den.

Shelby looked up at him. "You'll be done next week at this rate."

"What're you going to do with this stuff?"

"Take some of it. Goodwill's taking the rest."

He looked at the floor. "We could load it into the truck and take it out there soon as I'm done."

"I'll leave it outside for them."

"I wouldn't mind," he said.

"I don't really want to take a ride anywhere."

"I could take it myself."

Shelby stuffed paper towels around the dishes and said nothing.

Grimsley put his hands in his pockets, stood awhile, then went back to the bathroom.

He caulked the spaces between the boards, flattened the paste with the tips of his fingers. When he was done, he carved his mother's initials into a corner of the wood, which he always did when he completed a job. He didn't wait for the caulk to dry. He stapled the remainder of the plastic over the wood and pressed it flat against the caulk so it would hold. Afterward, he cleaned out the tub and put his tools in order.

Outside, he set the ladder against the house and climbed up. He wrapped some insulation in plastic and stuffed it inside the hole. Then he went back to his trailer and looked through the pile of old junk he kept behind the house. He sifted through some rotten logs, an old radio, some broken birdhouses, some engine parts—a carburetor, a water pump, half a fender—and found a thin piece of sheet metal. It began to snow again. He took the slot of metal back to the woman's trailer and fixed it over the hole in the roof with his hand drill. Climbing down, he stood in the snow and watched the door to the trailer, listened for movement inside, watched his white breath in the air. Then he picked up the ladder, his toolbox, and walked home.

Mona listened to him with her arms crossed. "You're an old fool," she said.

Shelby finished packing her grandmother's things. She rolled up clothes, wrapped the woman's jewelry in plastic wrap, set them all in a paper bag in her suitcase. She found a slingshot at the top of the closet, and a pair of men's underwear. She looked for letters but found none. A stack of newspaper clippings about tornadoes was in a box under the bed, and a book about Australia. In the center of the book, Shelby examined pictures of aboriginal boys and girls, their faces painted in reds and whites, their joints like knotted spools. She studied the photos of the coastline, the wasteland of the desert, kangaroos, and rats, a man with tooth marks down his arm from a crocodile. The man seemed proud.

She found a collection of scented candles in another box, covered over with a thick, green army blanket. Among the woman's files and bills she found some cartoons and a drawing that Shelby had made with crayons when she was younger: a church with a dog on the steeple. In a white envelope she found a picture of a naked young man.

Afterward, she packed up her own things, leaving her toothbrush, some clothes, and her book and journal on the kitchen counter. She set a pot of water to boil and opened the book. She wrote.

When we left Kitty Hawk at the end of 1901, we doubted that we would ever resume our experiments. Although we had broken the record for distance in gliding, and although Mr. Chanute, who was present at the time, assured us that our results were better than had ever before been attained, yet when we looked at the time and money which we had expended, and considered the progress made and the distance yet to go, we considered our experiments a failure. At this time I made the prediction that men will sometime fly, but that it would not be within our lifetime.

When the tea had boiled, Shelby found a mug in one of the boxes and poured herself a cup. She began copying the passage into her notebook. When a knock came at the window, she set the book aside and went to the door.

"You're to come for dinner," Grimsley said. "And to stay over too. No sense in staying alone tonight."

"I like it alone."

"Well, if you don't come, I'm going to be in a lot of trouble."

Shelby looked at him. "Your trouble is not my concern."

He was glad of her tone. He could go now, and it would not be held against him. He was glad to be done with this girl.

"I know what you're feeling," he said. "When I'm hurt I want nobody about me, cause I don't want them to see me hurt, and it's none of their damn business anyways. People seeing me hurt just gets me more hurt. What's the point, you know? Does that sound right to you?"

She nodded. "Something like that."

"Well, that's not good thinking," said Grimsley. "This is not a world to go alone in, and today's not a day to stay alone. I'm afraid for you, and my wife is afraid for you. We'd like you to come stay with us tonight. Do you understand what I'm saying?"

Shelby blinked. "I didn't know you were going to get all worked up."

"I'm not worked up," said Grimsley.

"Right," said Shelby. "What time?"

She'd annoyed him again. "What time what?" he said.

The girl said nothing.

"Oh," said Grimsley.

In the evening, they drove the truck out to the bay, passing the lines of boats tied to the docks, the empty masts lined in rows like candles. Two women stood on a sandbar, casting their lines out into the surf. Long shadows stretched from the tree line. Shelby sat between Grimsley and Mona, moving her knees to the side every time Grimsley shifted gears. She kept her eyes down and picked at the tips of her fingers. Mona had packed dinner in a basket.

"Do you know your sister very well?" she asked Shelby.

"Not really."

"Does she have a family?"

"No."

Mona nodded. "Well it'll just be the two of you, then."

"Yes, ma'am."

A flock of gulls scattered as Grimsley pulled into the parking lot. Out past the schooners, the red light of a buoy could be seen near the mouth of the cove. The light bobbed and dipped with the current.

Grimsley helped the two women onto the trawler, put some oil into the engine, started it up. A cloud of black smoke blew out of the pipe, and the deck hummed under their feet. Outside, he scraped the ice off the cabin windows, and inside Mona got the heat going, set a pot of water to boil on the tiny burner. Shelby sat on the bench near the wheel, stared out onto the black water. She could see the reflection of white clouds, a few stars. Grimsley untied the line and switched on the running lights. He took the wheel in the cabinhouse, peered out into the dark, opened the throttle a bit. The trawler pushed out past the dock and the other vessels, moved into the bay.

"I'll let you take the wheel in a while if you're up to it," said Grimsley.

"Okay," said Shelby.

"You been on the water before?"

"No."

Mona opened the basket and took out a thick candle. She set it in the center of the chart table and lit it. The tiny glow reflected off the port windows, seemed to sit out on the water. Foil wrappers and plastic containers of food were set on the table, plates on three sides after that. Forks and knives soon after. Through the planking, they could hear the lap of the water over the hum of the engine.

"Well," said Mona, "we need to eat before all this gets cold."

Grimsley took the trawler out a little farther, headed toward the buoy and the reflection of stars in the water. Mona served slices of turkey and gravy, some vegetables onto their plates. After he dropped anchor, they settled around the table.

Tea was poured, and Grimsley began eating. Shelby looked at her plate and closed her eyes.

"You not hungry?" he said.

"I don't like to eat in front of people."

Grimsley looked over at his wife.

"Why's that?"

Shelby shrugged. "I get sick."

"You do whatever's comfortable," said Mona.

Grimsley kept his eyes on his plate as he ate. He'd heard some strange things in this life—he had his own strange things, he knew—but he'd not heard this before.

"Maybe I'll eat something later," said Shelby.

"Whatever you want," said Mona.

"I know that's rude."

"Nonsense."

They ate in silence, and Grimsley looked up at his wife every once in a while. The water was calm in the bay, and the vessel rocked slowly in the current. A little tea was spilled on the table. When the candle went out, the flame dipped into wax, they didn't light it again. They sat in the shadows cast by the bulbs outside, the sky's reflection on the water.

Shelby put her elbows on the table. "Can I ask you something?"

Mona looked up from her plate. "Sure."

"Don't look."

The woman smiled and dropped her eyes. "All right."

"What happened to your arm?"

The woman pulled her sleeve to her wrist, covered the burn.

"Sorry," said Shelby.

"No, that's all right." She kept her eyes on her plate. "There was a fire downstairs when I was a teenager. I was about sixteen or so. My father was drinking, and it got started, and it burned the house down. I woke up and I was burning. I opened up the window and got out. That's all."

"Did he get out?"

"No," Mona said. "He and my mother and my sister didn't make it out. The fire moved pretty quickly. It wasn't that good of a house."

"And you were sixteen?"

"That's right."

Shelby stared down at the food on her plate. "Where'd you go?"

"Well, believe it or not I stayed with a group of nuns for a while. I didn't have any family, and that's where the state put me until I was eighteen. That was an experience."

"Did they try to convert you?" said Shelby. She was interested in this story.

"No," said Mona. "Honestly, I think they were glad to get rid of me. But they fed me and gave me a roof over my head and taught me some discipline. There was one nun, Sister Marilynn, and she and I kept up till she died a few years back. I don't remember knowing her that well when I was there, but she became important later. Her family actually put me through two years of college."

"Did you finish?" said Shelby.

"Careful," said Grimsley to Mona. "This is her favorite question."

Mona smiled as if she were in on the joke. "No. I met Grimsley then.

And when I met Grimsley a lot of things ended and a lot of things began for me."

"That sounds like a loaded statement," said Grimsley.

"Oh, it is," said Mona. "I'll keep my room to maneuver."

She had met him in the prison where he served for six years. After he'd killed his two friends in the accident. He worked in the prison office on Fridays, and they had gotten to passing notes. It had seemed dangerous and thrilling to Mona at the time, though she was not now sure in reflection. That time came back to her now. She looked over at Grimsley. That had been many choices ago.

"You are going to have a wonderful time on the West Coast," said Mona. "There is so much to see there."

"I don't think so," said Shelby.

"You've got an exciting life ahead of you," said Mona. "Doesn't she, Grimsley?"

He nodded. "We went through the coast of Washington on the way to Alaska every summer. How many years did we do that?"

"Nine years," said Mona.

"You have to take the ferryboat through the Inside Passage," he said. "You'll see amazing things."

"Bears and dolphins," said Mona.

"Not together, though," said Grimsley.

"The northern lights," said Mona.

"Those are at night," said Grimsley.

"She knows that," said Mona. "She's not a ninny."

Shelby picked up her mug, sipped at the cold tea. Grimsley and Mona finished their dinner. Through the windows of the cabin they could see the glow of the moon behind the clouds. The dark waves rippled in the light.

"I'm afraid," said Shelby.

"Of course you are," said Mona. "That's perfectly normal."

"I don't feel perfectly normal," said Shelby.

Grimsley looked at his wife. He wished he had better luck. Like a working brain or a wisdom that came from experience. Instead he seemed to have his endless confusion. He wished he had something better to share with those around him.

"You're going to see all these little golf balls in trees," he said.

Shelby looked at him. "What are you talking about?"

"Little golf balls," he said. He looked out the porthole. "Hundreds of them in the trees it'll look like. When you visit Alaska. You can see them from the ferryboat. But when you get closer you'll see that they're the heads of bald eagles. Maybe not hundreds of them. But close. You'll have never seen anything like it. All these bald eagles in the trees."

Mona looked at him, surprised. He hadn't spoken this much in years. He went on.

"And when you see those," he said, "things will be a lot better than they are now. Things don't always stay this way. You'll see those bald eagles and you'll remember us, telling you this. You probably won't remember our names, but that's okay. You'll be a lot better, and all this stuff you're feeling will seem very far away."

Shelby placed her hands on the table. She took up a napkin and blew her nose. Another trawler passed them by outside, this one coming into shore, and they bobbed in its wake.

"I'll remember your names," she said.

Now, there are two ways of learning how to ride a fractious horse. One is to get on him and learn by actual practice how each motion and trick may be best met; the other is to sit on a fence and watch the beast awhile, and then retire to the house and at leisure figure out the best way of overcoming his jumps and kicks. The latter system is the safest; but the former, on the whole, turns out the larger proportion of good riders. It is very much the same in learning to ride a flying machine; if you are looking for perfect safety, you will do well to sit on the fence and watch the birds; but if you really wish to learn, you must mount a machine and become acquainted with its tricks by actual trial.

In her memory, Shelby thinks of her hands on the wheel of the trawler, turning the point of the bow into the waves, pulling back on the throttle. In the spotlight, white mist from the water floated in the glow. They'd

gone out beyond the cove, Grimsley pointing out the crab traps and the
shallow reef hidden on the port side. In the bay, they'd pushed the throttle
forward, skipped across the whitecaps, kept their eyes on the blue-black
water. Orange jugs floated in the moonlight, and a tanker moved slowly
across the horizon, an irregular shadow across the long flat water. Shelby
had wanted to move out farther, perhaps circle the vessel.

"It'd take all night," said Grimsley.

But they'd gone anyway, the trawler dipping and rolling in the open
ocean. The tanker moved faster the closer they came, across the horizon
and north toward Wilmington. Shelby looked out through the fogged
window. At some point, she knew they'd never reach it.

"Gas'll run short," said Grimsley.

"A little longer."

"It's your swim back."

When they'd turned around, Grimsley let her keep the wheel, into the
bay, and then past the shallows, into the cove. Mona's eyes closed as she
sat on the bench, slept little, rolling and dipping with the waves. On the
far shoreline, they could make out a campfire on the beach, a half-dozen
figures kneeling in the white-orange glow. Shelby guided the vessel
around a stretch of fisherman's netting. Grimsley mumbled directions,
watched her hand on the throttle. She eased the boat into the berth, past
the other trawlers, the crab boats. She brought the vessel level with the
dock. Took her time, cut the engine.

Outside, Grimsley kicked the ice off the bow, crouched at the rail-
ing, felt a sting of ice in his knee, then in his belly. He was unsure of the
source. He was an old fool, he was sure, looked at his own reflection in
the water. Any light in a rooster's eyes, other than the sun, was bad business. Had that been his mother's? He wasn't sure. He took the ratline in
his fist, reached for the dock. Too much good luck was bad luck, but no
bad luck was always good luck. He was sure of that, felt the ice melt and
sting in his belly.

He had his favorites too, but he'd not yet had cause to use them all.
Don't litter. Leave sleeping cats alone. To keep evil spirits away, drop

some burnt cinders into your shirt pocket. And if you find a stranger's wallet, always take a dollar before returning it. Then, give that dollar to another stranger. It will bring all three of you good luck. Grimsley caught the dock with the tips of his fingers, kept the line from touching the water, and wrapped it around the wooden bollard.

COYOTES

Nate and Merrill fussed about in the kitchen. The boy was seventeen, the girl almost sixteen, and their father sat at the kitchen table repairing a clock that a neighbor had brought to him. He was almost seventy, the father, and had long been deaf. His heart was weak now, and he was no longer able to work as a fisherman, as he had for the whole of his life. There were filets of cobia baking in the oven, and asparagus and corn frying on the stove. The boy concentrated on assembling a salad: they'd been heavy on the vegetables lately. They were good for the father's heart. The man searched among the parts spread out on the table: the gears, the recoils, the pin and escape wheels, though he could not find the switch he was looking for. A wave of heavy rain washed over the house, then died away, leaving a steady, irregular patter. It was early autumn, and the edge of a hurricane had passed through the harbor town. They'd spent the afternoon waiting for the walls of their trailer to collapse. The boy, then the girl had signed to their father. *Bad rain*, or *Heavy wind*, or *This is the worst now*, and he'd signed back. *I cannot hear, but I can feel.*

He had a strange sign, the old man. Formal and slow. He did not touch his body when he signed, and he looked up at them now, banged his knuckles on the table to get their attention. *If the traps are washed away, we cannot afford to replace them.*

We know this, signed the boy, and then he said something to his sister that the man could not make out. *Why do you tell us things we know already?*

The money is short here, the man signed back. *There is nothing else worth speaking of.*

The girl set the wooden fork aside and signed at her father. Her sign was slow as well, but complicated. She touched her face and chest often as she signed. *You will get the boat back in the spring. Then Nate and I will fish. How do you fit many worries into a small head?*

Look at my head, signed the man. *There is nothing small about it.*

This set the boy and the girl to laughing, and the man smiled a little, went back to his clock. They filled the plates and set them on the table. The boy moved the pieces of clock to the side in sets of two and in the same order, and the old man watched him carefully. The bank had foreclosed on his trawler, and he believed it dishonest. He believed many things dishonest, and he'd been bitter and short with his children of late. He looked at the plate of food. He was a fisherman, and here he was, tired of fish.

What is with you two? he signed. *Why do we eat early tonight?*

The traps, the boy signed. *You worry over the traps all day. We go to check the traps so you will not worry. Now eat.* The boy put his fingers to his mouth. *Eat now.*

The man pushed his plate away. *I don't want to eat. I am not your child.*

Yes you are, signed the boy.

Papa, the girl signed. She placed her hand at the old man's elbow and looked at him. *Your heart.*

They will wash out to sea, signed the man.

The boy rolled his eyes. He put an asparagus in his mouth. *Shh,* he said. *Listen to your mother. Eat.*

The old man looked at his plate. He was very tired. He thought, as he often did, that if he went to sleep he would not wake up again. He had built the crab traps himself, and they were tied smartly, and with enough slack, to the buoys. He hoped they would be all right. They had survived storms worse than this one. He worried that they would be carried to the other side of the sound.

The boy put his fork down, as if reading his father's thoughts. *They will not get the traps,* he signed. *Those people. They take everything from us. But they will not get the traps.*

The old man looked at his son. He took a long breath. *What people?* signed the old man. *Who takes what from us?*

You know, the boy signed. He tapped his fingers angrily at his forehead. He pointed out the window, across the sound. *They have everything and we have nothing.*

The old man shook his head. He was sad for the boy, though he did not say this. He cut off a piece of cobia, then ate it.

Their children are worse, the boy continued. He signed very quickly. *We hear them in school. What they own. What they do not. What they will own.*

The old man looked out the window at the rain. It was slow now, and the storm was coming to an end. The man thought of the way his son had pointed across the sound. The motion frightened him. He could see his own anger in the anger of the boy. It was something that had arisen recently and fully. The man tapped his knife at his plate.

This is very good, he signed. *They cannot get cobia like this across the sound.*

They buy the best fish, signed the boy. He was still very angry, and he was looking out the window.

The old man touched the boy's chin. It was unusual for him to do this. *Listen to me,* he signed. *You will come to market with me again. You forget. We sell them only the bad fish.* The man made a funny face, as if he'd swallowed something distasteful.

The boy said nothing. He continued eating. The sacks for the crabs were set by the door, next to the long raincoats that the boy and girl wore out on the boat.

What will you two do tonight? the man signed.

We have told you, signed the boy. He signed lazily, as if they were half-words. *We check the traps.*

After, said the man. *I think you are up to something.*

We are up to nothing, signed the boy.

The man looked at his daughter, and the girl looked down at her plate. She was quiet, that one, when she chose to be, and she was not yet filled with anger.

I know my own children, the man signed.

They settled their father in front of the television after dinner. They placed a beer in his hands, though he was only allowed the one. Merrill placed a blanket over him and tucked it into the cushions of the chair. There was a special on the television about coyotes. They watched for a while, and Merrill could hear Nate rummaging around in the back room. She signed for her father, for what the woman was saying on television.

They are two times the size of foxes, she signed.

I can see this, the man signed. *Does she think we are stupid?*

There might be a blind person listening, the girl signed, and the man said nothing to that. He looked irritated, but he was happy. She still had a kindness that ran deep in her.

They hunt in pairs, signed the girl. *Half die before they are adults.*

Why? signed the man.

Merrill smiled. *I did not hear*, she signed. *The woman talks too fast. Their territory grows. It grows now. They howl to speak to other coyotes.* There was not a sign she knew for coyotes, so she spelled it out, quickly.

Who else would they speak with? the man signed. *This woman has no sense in her head.*

Nate came into the room and stood watching the television with them. He had his raincoat in his hand and a small paper bag that he stuffed into one of the pockets. *Those are nasty creatures*, he signed.

They are very smart, signed the old man.

The boy spelled a word out. *Scavengers*, he signed. *They eat children.*

No they don't, signed the man. *They eat rats and rabbits.*

I have heard them at night, signed the boy. *Here. Out in the woods.*

No you haven't, signed the man.

The boy looked at his father. *How would you know?* he signed.

The man looked again at the television. He took a swig from his beer. His feelings were hurt, though he would not show the boy this. *You have heard dogs*, he signed.

I know things, signed the boy.

I know you do, signed the old man.

The girl pointed at the television. She struggled for a moment, trying to find the right sign. Then she pointed again. *They eat frogs,* she signed. *This is what was just said.*

The boy and the girl took the old rowboat out into the sound. The patches in the boat were poor, and Merrill bailed with an old milk jug while Nate pulled at the oars. The sky had begun to clear, and the water seemed a dark and strange blue. There was old trash and netting out on the water, things that had blown out with the wind, and the clouds and stars reflected on the choppy surface of the water as if they were slowly moving in toward shore. The moon was low and crescent, a half, though a large one, and Nate rowed with it over his shoulder. They headed out toward the traps and shared a beer on the way, their feet cold and wet with the water leaked through.

When they came to the buoys, they pulled the traps up, and some were empty and some were filled with one or three or half a dozen crabs, but they did not empty the traps and instead dropped them back into the water. Two of the lines were broken, and they would come back tomorrow, dive down into the cold water, pull back to the surface what was theirs. They headed now across the sound, toward the large houses, toward the lanterns strung all across the docks there like a long line of spider eyes in the distance, not menacing but watching. Nate had his hood up over his head, and Merrill watched the tip of his nose, the moustache below that he'd been trying to grow. They were best friends and didn't have many others in school.

"I got it," the boy said.

"You got what?"

"The job on the ferry. Permanent now. It's twenty hours. I'll start on Tuesday."

She was happy for him, but also sad. He'd no longer be working at the grocery store with her. "Can you get me a job there?"

He shook his head, leaned into the oars. "You're too young."

"I'm mature for my age though," she said.

He watched her bail the water. "No you're not," he said. "You're not mature at all."

"Example," she said.

He thought about that. They were past the halfway point in the sound. He looked back at the houses across the way. "You couldn't watch me shoot William," he said.

Merrill frowned at that. She didn't like to think much about that. "I was right there when you shot William."

"You closed your eyes though."

"I closed his eyes first," she said.

William had been their mule. They'd used him when they went apple picking, a job they'd had since they were very young. He'd follow them along in the orchard, two baskets tied across his back. He'd gotten too old, and his legs had begun to go. They'd shot him at the edge of the orchard, at the end of last season. They'd shot him first, then dug the hole for him, and it upset her, Merrill, to think of it. Though, it would've been worse the other way. The farmer had told them it was past time, that it was long past time, that there was no sense in these sentimental ideas. Still, he brought the mule a pear that morning, offering it silently and rubbing down the animal's coat.

They moved along on the water, dipping and rolling with the tide. The ferryboat ran across in place of a bridge. They could see it now, off in the distance, a ten-minute ride that people across the sound seemed to like.

"I'm happy for you," said Merrill.

"Thanks."

"That is the big-time," she said.

The boy said nothing. He watched her, suspiciously.

"Now will you take people's money, or will you wave the cars on and off?"

He was still suspicious. "I'll do both."

"Both?" she said. "But someone's got to tie the line. Will you do that too?"

He splashed her with one of the oars, though she didn't blink.

"Do they have a knot that you're supposed to tie, or will you get to use your own?"

"I use my own," he said.

"Impressive. Is it complicated?"

"No," he said. "Any fool can do it. We call it the Merrill knot."

She ignored that. "Will you make change for people?"

"Why are you being all stupid?" he said.

"It's a dollar fifty now," she said. "Will you have one of those little tube things for the quarters, or will you just carry them loose in your pocket?"

"I'm going to carry them in a little bag and knock you upside the head when I get home."

Merrill said nothing to that. She looked up at the houses. They were almost there now. Nate also turned and looked. They could see the dock where they would land. There seemed to be no one about.

"Can I come visit with you?" Merrill said.

"On the ferry?"

"Yes."

"No," he said.

She smiled at that, looked forward to it. She set the bailer aside and picked up the sacks. There was one light on at the house up ahead. A kitchen light, the sort people leave on when they are away at night. It was a house that Merrill had studied for many Saturdays now.

"Did you bring the gun?" she said.

Nate looked back, pulled at the oars. He judged the distance, looked for any movement on shore.

"No," he said. "Why would I bring the gun?"

The girl said nothing, and the boy shook his head. He watched the kitchen light.

"There's no reason to bring the gun," he said.

They pulled the boat up, not to the dock, but into the tall reeds and under the darkness of a sycamore that was growing crooked over the water. There was a tire and rope—a swing—tied to the tree, and it was wrapped and wrapped around the thick branch. By human hand or wind they did not know. They tied the boat up, then waited there and watched the house. There were a dozen windows at the back, but only the one light on in the kitchen, and there was a long deck made of wood and a large garden filled with bright plants and flowers. Some of the planters had been knocked over by the storm, and the birdbath was nestled sideways against a rosebush.

There was a thick line of trees on either side of the yard, so that they could not see the neighbor's houses or even any light from there. He'd worked some Saturdays on the ferry, Nate had, and he knew the couple that lived here. They went across the water each Saturday and did not return till late. Each night he'd seen them they were dressed up, and he'd often imagined the parties they went to. Candles and a ballroom, men smoking and women drinking from tiny glasses. Foolish thoughts of his, he knew. He'd only seen movies. But that was how he thought of these people. He watched for a dog or for any sign of movement. The driveway was long and winding, and they could barely hear the cars up on the road. They listened to the wind, and to a howling down the shoreline. One coyote howled, and then another. The sound—shrill and curious—carried along the water, and when they'd gone silent again Nate picked up the sacks from the bottom of the boat and stepped up onto the grass.

They walked up the yard slowly and silently. They found the garage unlocked with three spaces inside. No cars there. They climbed over the fence to the yard, as if this was the most normal thing to do, and they made their way up the deck and to the back door. Here Nate knelt on one knee and took the picks out from the paper bag. He was good with mechanical things. Merrill stood watch, looking out across the backyard. The view was not unlike the view from the other side. The moonlight stretched across the sound, and the water seemed blue and dark, the waves rippling across the way. The lights on the Coast Guard buoys ticked red and then disappeared, and then red again, and she could make out the ferry, way off in the distance: the white running lights and its slow push toward the mainland.

The lock popped open, and they went inside and closed the door. The air smelled of coffee and a strange perfume, and Nate flipped on the light and they squinted in the brightness.

The room was long and the ceilings high, and there were two couches and many chairs, all of white leather, and a long staircase led upstairs. A dining room was set off in an alcove, and there were plates and silverware set out, as if a meal was about to be served. There were two fireplaces, one on either side of the long room, and the brickwork had been painted black and it led up in a funnel all the way to the ceiling. Merrill picked up a book from the coffee table, a photo book about Europe, and there was an ashtray there, in the shape of a swan, and a decanter filled with whiskey or scotch. Nate walked about the kitchen, running his hand along the marble countertop and touching the toaster, which was small and made of aluminum, and it seemed the same as the one they had at home.

"Do you want a drink?" said Merrill.

"All right," he said.

She poured the scotch into two glasses and they toasted but said nothing. They sipped their drinks slowly and each made a face as they swallowed.

They took their sacks and went upstairs. They'd agreed beforehand to look for jewelry and money. They went into a room that was obviously an office, and there was a big oaken desk set in the center of the room and photographs, black-and-white, set on blue backgrounds, no glass, on the walls. The photographs were of landscapes: rivers and tobacco fields and a strange, distant shot of the ocean with two figures standing out in the water. Nate took his pocketknife out and cut through the picture of the river. He tore it diagonally, and the paper flapped back like a wave.

"Stop that," the girl said.

"Fuck them," he said. "They don't own the water."

"Use your head," she said.

He ripped his knife through the tobacco fields, then the ocean. He kicked the chair over, then knocked the pens and notebooks off the desk.

There was a half-bottle of red wine sitting on a cabinet, and he took the cork out and poured the wine on the carpet. He tossed the bottle out into the hallway. It knocked against the banister and then rolled away.

"You are such a boy," Merrill said.

He wiped his lips with his sleeve. "Yes, I am a boy," he said.

"Aim high," she said. "Become something better."

They went into the largest room, a bedroom, and they opened the drawers and found the jewelry: necklaces and rings, and a little pendant ringed with diamonds. Two bracelets with a stone they didn't know. They stuffed these into one of the sacks, and they opened one of the closets.

They searched slowly. The closet was filled with dresses and sweaters, and they searched through pockets and hems. They reached up to the boxes on the shelves. Shoes inside this one, papers in another.

The smallest box was filled with money: fives and twenties and fifties, crisp and new, and Nate dropped the box whole into the sack.

"Idiots," he said. "They deserve what they get." He looked at the dresses. He pointed at them. "Take them."

"I don't want dresses," said Merrill.

"Yes you do," the boy said.

They opened the other closet, and it was empty. There were square patches of dust on the shelves, as if something had been there recently, and the bar was filled with hangers, set for shirts on one side and cardboard slats for pants on the other. A single sock—black with blue stripes at the top—lay in the corner. They picked it up and studied it, as if it might contain some value.

"We'll have another drink," said Merrill. "Then we'll go."

"Take the dresses," said Nate.

The girl looked at them. They were mostly dark—blues, blacks, and reds—but there was one, gray with red stitching at the collar, that she admired. She took it from the hanger and held it up against her shoulders. She could smell the perfume of the woman upon it.

"Will it fit?" she said.

"Take it," said Nate.

"I'll put it on," she said.

He shrugged, looked into the sack. "Live it up."

She went into the bathroom and put the dress on over her clothes. There was a man she had in mind, a man who she'd guessed was twenty-eight. He'd often shop at the grocery store where she worked on weekends. He had a beard and would often talk with her when she put his beer, his vegetables, into paper sacks. There was something formal about him, perhaps something friendly behind it, and she wondered what he would think of this dress. She looked in the mirror and patted it down along her stomach. She turned off the light and stood in the dark for a moment, then she went out into the room.

"Movie star," said Nate. "That is all you."

"I don't care for the movies," she said.

"Don't you?"

"Amateurs, all of them," she said. "I have a beautiful voice. They don't let you sing in the movies anymore."

"Let's hear it," said Nate.

She shook her head, looked down at her dress. "You'll have to pay."

"I'm cheap," he said. "I'll give you five dollars for a dance."

"I don't want your money," she said, but she held her hand against her chest, and the other outstretched at her side, as if she had a partner there. Her mother—Nate's mother—had been a good dancer, and she'd taught her the waltz among others. Merrill moved to it now. She imagined the man from the grocery store as her partner. Imagined him formal and elegant. Imagined the music about her. She moved to it, moved across the room.

"You're a freak," said Nate.

"Shh," she said. She moved to the corner of the bed, then spun away. She moved in a circle near the doorway, allowed herself a dip. She could hear her brother laugh. She closed her eyes, and soon after, she ran into the wall. She listened for his laugh. She opened her eyes. He was looking at her, smiling. He'd allow her this moment.

She spun out into the hallway, dipped again. She felt the same—elegant and formal—as her imagined partner. She took another dip. Did a curtsey. The next song was not a waltz, and she decided to leave the dance floor. She bowed and looked down the hallway.

There was a little girl standing there. She wore a pajama top and shorts and looked to be about eight years old. She held a hand on the banister and one foot on top of the other. She smiled at Merrill as if she'd expected her to be there all along.

"Hi," the girl said.

"Hi," said Merrill.

"You mustn't wear my mother's dress."

Merrill looked down at the dress. She flattened down the stomach. The wine bottle had rolled into the middle of the hallway, halfway to the girl.

"I'm sorry," said Merrill.

"We're not to touch her things."

"No," said Merrill. "We shouldn't do that."

"Why not?" said Nate. He'd come to the door and was staring down at the girl.

"Because we mess them up."

"We won't mess them up," he said.

The girl considered that. She had a strange way about her. Her movements were like those of someone older. Before she spoke she tucked her hair behind her ears.

"Maybe you're old enough," she said.

"We're plenty old," he said.

"When I'm old enough I'll be able to touch them."

"You can touch her things now," he said.

Merrill looked at him. "Stop it," she said.

"You stop it."

"I'm to get a dog," the girl said. "If I keep quiet at night and don't bother things. If I'm very good, I'm to get a dog. Do you have a dog?"

"No," said Merrill.

"You must not be very good then," said the girl.

"No," said Nate. "We're very bad."

Merrill looked at him again. He had a tone in his voice that she didn't like. "I mean it," she said.

"Fuck off."

"Oh," the girl said. She covered her mouth as if she'd been the one that said it.

Merrill didn't take her eyes off her brother. She signed to him quickly. She often signed when she was angry. *Stop it*, she signed. *Don't scare this girl. I'm not going to tell you again.*

He frowned and looked down the stairs. "Let's go," he said.

"You'll have to put the dress back," said the girl.

Merrill looked at the girl. "Yes. We're going to put it back now. Just like we found it, and no one will have to know."

"I won't tell," said the girl.

"You're a very good girl," said Merrill. "You go back to bed now, and we'll put this back, and then we're going to leave."

The girl looked at the floor. She pulled her hair behind her ears. "All right," she said, and she went back to her room.

Merrill picked up the wine bottle from the floor and went back into the bedroom. She took the dress off carefully. The dress smelled of perfume and smoke. She picked up the sack, took out the jewelry, and put it back in the drawer, and then she looked in the sack at the box of money. Their father was very sick, and he needed the heart medicine. She dumped the money into the sack, but put the box back where they'd found it. She put the other boxes back too and then hung the dress on a hanger. She pulled the bedspread tight so there would be no wrinkles in it. Then she turned out the light, put the empty wine bottle into the sack, and went into the hallway.

Nate wasn't there. She looked down the staircase. She could see the coffee table and the decanter and the book and the swan. She walked down to the girl's room and went in. The room was very large and there were many shelves of books on the wall. There were no toys or posters. Nate was standing at the girl's window, across the room from her, looking outside toward the water. The girl was sitting up in bed, studying him.

"What are you doing?" Merrill said.

"I'm not doing anything," said Nate.

"You're going to scare her," she said.

He turned and looked at his sister. He shrugged and didn't say anything.

"He's going to leave," said the girl.

"Yes," said Merrill. "We're both going to leave."

"No," said the girl. "He's going to leave you. If you argue like that. You mustn't argue so much."

Merrill looked at her brother. He put his hands in his pockets.

"I'm not going to leave her," he said. "It's okay to argue sometimes."

"It's not ever okay," said the girl. "That's how the men leave."

Nate smiled at that. "Don't believe everything you hear."

The girl cleared her throat. "Has anyone ever told you that you are quite handsome?"

This made both Nate and Merrill laugh. Such an odd tone in the girl's voice.

"It sounds like you've been practicing that," said Nate.

The girl nodded. "My mother said that to a man who was not my father."

They didn't say anything to that.

"Did you put the dress back?" the girl said. She was looking at Merrill.

"Yes," said Merrill. She pointed to Nate. "I don't think he's all that handsome. He's kind of funny-looking, don't you think?"

"Nice," said Nate.

The girl stared up at them. She put her fingers up to the edge of the covers.

"You'd better be careful," she said.

"I don't want to be careful," said Merrill. "He's funny-looking. I want to hear you say it."

"No," said the girl.

"Yes," said Merrill.

The girl looked at Nate. She pulled the covers up an inch. She smiled and tucked her hair back behind her ears.

"He's a little funny-looking."

Nate rolled his eyes. He looked incredibly young to Merrill when he did that.

The girl pulled her arms from under the covers. She flattened the covers down.

"Does your father like him?" she said. She was looking over at Merrill.

"Of course," said Merrill.

"That's very important," the girl said. "What is he like?"

"My father?"

"Yes," said the girl. "I should be quiet."

Merrill leaned into the doorway. She looked back behind her, down the stairs. "He's a small man, but he has a big head," she said.

"Very big?" said the girl.

"Very, very big," said Merrill. She held her hands out from her ears for a moment, making an enormous head. "He's quiet, and he's sick. He has trouble with his heart."

"What kind of trouble?"

Merrill looked at her brother. He was staring at the sack in her hand, and he tapped his fingers twice against his wrist, though there was no watch there.

"Two minutes," she said to him, then she looked at the girl. "It doesn't work right. He needs some medicine so it will tick right again."

"Is it broken?" said the girl.

"No," said Merrill.

"What does it sound like, when it's not ticking right?"

Merrill smiled at that. She looked back behind her. Down the stairs. "It's probably a little off."

"And will you give him the medicine?"

"Yes. We'll give it to him tomorrow."

"And will that fix it?"

"Yes," said Merrill.

"I'm glad."

Merrill nodded at her. "I'll tell him you said that."

"Please do," said the girl. "Do you hear the dogs out there?"

They listened for them. They held still and listened. They could hear the coyotes howling off in the distance. It was very faint, but they could hear it.

"We hear them," said Nate.

"If I'm very good I'll get a dog," said the girl.

"I'm sure it will be a very nice dog," he said.

"They are very well behaved if you pick the right one," she said. "And they are very handsome to look at."

"That's right," said Nate.

"Have you seen them?"

The boy pointed at the window. "Those dogs?"

"Yes."

"I have," he said. "They're just as you said."

"Handsome?"

"Very much so," he said.

The girl looked out the window. The clouds had cleared, and the moon and the stars made a blue light.

"I saw you in the boat," the girl said. "I was supposed to stay in bed, but I didn't. I saw you come across in the boat."

Nate looked at her. He breathed in deeply. He'd been talking about dogs, but his mind was on his father.

"That's not how you get a dog," he said.

"No," said the girl. "You've got to stay in the bed."

They heard the key in the lock downstairs, a turn of the switch, then someone stumbling in. Merrill looked down the stairs. She saw the mother standing there, as if the woman were regaining her balance. She was dressed in a white dress, and she had dark hair. The woman ran her hands through it.

"Quiet," said the girl, and she held her finger up to her lips.

The woman came upstairs. She took a long time coming up the stairs. She stood there for a moment, looking down the hallway.

"Nadia?" she said.

The girl sat up in bed. "Yes?"

"I need you," said the woman.

The girl got out of the bed. She went out into the hallway and followed her mother into the bedroom. The woman stood facing the bed, and she pointed back to the zipper of her dress. The girl unzipped it, let the dress fall to the floor, and her mother stepped out of it. She pulled back the covers, the mother did, and slipped into bed.

Nadia took the dress and shook it once. Then again. She pulled up a chair. She found a hanger in the closet, next to the dress that the beautiful girl had worn. The dress had no wrinkles and had been hung correctly. She closed the closet and looked at her mother. She turned out the light.

"Did you see Father tonight?" said the girl.

"I saw him."

"Was he well?"

"He was very well."

The girl stood at the edge of the bed. She could hear the boy and the girl walk past in the hallway.

"I've had a very exciting evening," she said.

"Well that makes one of us," said the woman.

The girl waited there. She listened to the boy and the girl walk down the stairs. Heard them open the door and go out. She imagined the boat in her mind. She walked around and stood next to the bed. Her mother smelled of alcohol and smoke. The girl wondered what her heart sounded like.

"Who's the best dancer?" said the girl.

"You are," said the woman.

The girl waited to be let into the bed. She wanted to go look out the window, but she stood there instead. She waited.

They untied the boat from the tree and pushed out into the water. Merrill took the oars this time, and Nate sat at the stern of the boat. He held the sack in his hands. The half-moon was high and it left a strange blue glow across the water. The ferryboat was out again, making its last run to the mainland. There were a few lights on their father's side of the sound. The water rippled against the boat, and above that sound they could hear the coyotes. The creatures were closer this time, as if they were just on the edge of the shore. Nate looked there, tried to make out the shapes in the moonlight.

He stood up in the boat and cupped his hands around his mouth. He took a breath and howled back to them, high first, then low, and his howl trailed off across the water, as if what he'd said had been a question. The echo sounded against the trees.

"Sit down," said Merrill. "Don't be foolish."

"Who will care about us?" he said. "Two trailer kids?"

She was very angry then, Merrill. She set the oars in her lap and let the boat drift along the water. *Use your head,* she signed. She poked her fingers against her temple. She was very quick with her signing. *If you don't use your head that is all you will ever be.*

There is nothing wrong with what I am, he signed. *This is our water. We can go where we want.* He waved his hands across the sound.

You will go where you want, she signed. *That is what you mean.* She looked at him for a long time. They couldn't hear the coyotes anymore. She looked at him till he sat down in the boat.

What is wrong with you?

She signed very quickly at him. *You are nobody to me. You are leaving me and now you are nobody.*

He stared at her. He was very angry, and he put his hands together to sign. He tried to find the right sign, but he made no motion. The boat dipped in a wave, and Merrill took up the oars again.

She pulled them toward home. He tried to make out their lights on the other side of the sound. But they were too far away. He thought again about their father's heart. The boy opened the sack and looked inside. He put his hands down into the money and looked for the jewelry. He fished around in the money. The Coast Guard buoys were still a ways off, and they headed out toward them. The red lights ticked on and again, and the hurricane was hours past. The air smelled of ozone and the bottom of the sea.

He found the wine bottle in the sack, but nothing else. Merrill had put the jewelry back in the bedroom drawer. Nate took a breath. He took out the bottle and set it at the bottom of the boat. It floated there, and the water was ankle deep. He would have to start bailing soon, or they would sink to the bottom. The water was very deep where they were headed.

That is foolish, he signed. *I'm not going to leave you.*

Merrill didn't say anything.

You know who I am, he signed. *I have listened to you.*

Merrill watched him, watched the houses they were leaving in the distance, the dark water between. She watched the motion of her brother's hands in the strange blue light. He spelled out his name very carefully. *I am Nate,* he signed.

ACKNOWLEDGMENTS

I received a lot of help, from a lot of people, in a variety of ways, in writing this book. This list is long, yet each thank-you is sincere, and I am most grateful for your encouragement and support.

Thanks especially to Ann Fitzmaurice, David Roderick, Chellis Ying, Jim Shepner, Terry Cole, Helen Kealey, Jack Kealey, Kerri Kealey, Scott Hutchins, Glen La Barber, and Shaila Djurovich for all of their moral, literary, and spiritual support over the years.

Thank-you to the Stegner Fellowship Program at Stanford University, the Blue Mountain Center, and Intersection for the Arts for their financial support and belief in my writing.

Everyone at the University of Georgia Press has been so generous, gracious, and wise. I especially want to thank Nancy Zafris, the Flannery O'Connor Award series editor, who chose *Thieves I've Known*, and who gave expert and generous advice about the book throughout this process. Thanks very much to Jon Davies, my editor, who guided me smartly and deftly throughout this process and who made many very helpful suggestions about the text. Thanks also to Sydney Dupre, who enthusiastically and expertly represented the book within the press. Thanks also to Mindy Conner, Kaelin Broaddus, and Jane Kobres for their patient help and thoughtful attention.

I've worked at Stanford University, in one form or another, for more than ten years now, so there are many, many people to thank there. Two of my biggest supporters have been Eavan Boland and John L'Heureux, and I am deeply grateful and appreciative for all of their wise counsel and enthusiastic energy over the years. Thanks also especially to Tobias

Wolff, Ken Fields, Adam Johnson, Elizabeth Tallent, and David MacDonald for teaching me (and so many of us) about writing, teaching, and living. My colleagues at Stanford are an absolute joy to work with, so great thanks to Scott again, Shimon Tanaka, Bruce Snider, Maria Hummel, Molly Antopol, Keith Ekiss, Skip Horack, Sarah Frisch, Sara Michas-Martin, Harriet Clark, Kirstin Valdez Quade, John Evans, Stephanie Soileau, and Brittany Perham.

I have many, many reasons to thank our administrative staff at Stanford, both in ways known and I'm sure unknown to me, so special thanks to Christina Ablaza, Mary Popek, Krystal Griffiths, Dagmar Logie, Alyce Bolster, Judy Candell, Katie Dooling, Nelia Peralta, and Nicole Bridges.

Why is Stephen Elliott all the way down here? I'm sure I'm going to hear about that one. Stephen is a writer's writer and a friend's friend and has helped me out of many a jam in the past. At the very least he gets to share a paragraph with so many wonderful friends and supporters like Cathy Schlund-Vials, John Kavanagh, Sara Young, Mark Purcell, Rachel Richardson, Ben Peterson, Wendy McKennon, Isaac Fitzgerald, Eric and Ashly Morrison, Steadman Harrison, Alyssa Harrison, Kristen Bahman, Peggy Cartner, Bruce again, Lysley Tenorio, Doug Klesch, Dorothy Hans, Andrew Altschul, Robin Ekiss, and Julie Greicius. Thank-you very sincerely to each of you.

Over the years I've received so many smart comments and insights about these stories and other writings from friends in workshops at Stanford, the University of Massachusetts, and elsewhere. Thank you very much to Katharine Noel, Steve again, Lysley again, Andrew again, Otis Haschemeyer, Tom McNeely, Jack Livings, Tamara Guirado, Sam Michel, Noy Holland, Peggy Woods, Nick Montemarano, Susan Steinberg, Malena Watrous, Kaui Hemmings, Eric Puchner, Stephanie Reents, Felicia Ward, Scott again, Adam again, and Skip again.

Thank you also to a number of additional friends at Stanford who've been so supportive: Gavin Jones, Denise Gigante, Dan Colman, Liz Frith, Charlie Junkerman, Elana Hornstein, Megan Miller, Nick Jenkins, Saikat Majumdar, Judy Richardson, Ramon Saldivar, Andrea Lunsford, Jennifer

Summit, Dan Archer, Dan Klein, Matt Jockers, Jeremy Sabol, Scott Doorley, Laura McGrane, Bob Smith, Marissa Gemma, and of course Natalie Jabbar.

I'd love to list all of my students, but a few will have to stand in for the many. Thanks to Lucas Loredo, Lauren YoungSmith, Nik Sawe, Danielle Sheeler, Anneke Nelson, Max Doty, Vauhini Vara, Jess Goldman, Killeen Hanson, and Sara Buer.

Thank-you, very much, to so many members of my family who have been so supportive over the years, especially Edward Kealey, Robert Kealey, Don Kealey, Margaret Kealey, Donald Kealey, and Doreen Kealey, and all the members of the Kealey, Carroll, and Glynn families.

Thank-you to George Sembert, Doug again, Mike Kunow, Sallie Phillips, Tony Bila, Jim again, Terry again, Glen again, Dieter Tannert, Cameron Otzman, Dave Hunt, and Laurie Sandell. You know why.

Last call. Thanks to Genie and Jennifer Alexander, Lisa Watts, Bob Malekof, Brigitte Chauvigne, Rosemarie Murphy, Jessica Partch, Krysty Byrd and Matt Alper, Chris and Adrianna Kirkman, Allison Jones, Dawn McAvoy, Gravity Goldberg, Sara Houghteling, Aubrey Aldret, Seth Abramson, Susan and Ben Malikowski, Chris "Commish" Cooney, Jon Berry, all at Squeeze the Rock, Phil Knight, Peter Rock, Todd Pierce, Kristen Tracy, Chris Baty, Julie Rigaudiere, Minerva Hallacy, David Barker, Katie Boyle, Lyndon Rego, Michael Breen, Jory John, Jeff Hoffman, Tommy and Kelcie Beaver, Victoria Chang, Erica Rice, Nancy Harrison, Laura Crescimano, Kara Hammond, Meena Wilson, Channan Tigay, Rebecca Black, Catharine Fox, Christina Tran, "Handsome John" Lundberg, Joe Harrison, Jenny Zhang, Cheryl McGrath, Josh Tyree and Emily Mitchell, Alvaro Villanueva, Ninive Calegari, Dave Eggers, Naomi, Phil, J.R. and everyone in the Greensboro Dashers, and Christine Texiera for the peepers.

"Introduction, or Nobody" first appeared as "Nobody" in *The Rumpus* (2013). "From Bremerton" was originally published in *Ascent* 25.3 (Spring 2001). "The Lost Brother" appeared first in *Glimmer Train* (2013).

"Thieves I've Known" was originally published as "Bones" in *Prairie Schooner* 77.4 (Winter 2003) and later anthologized in *Best American Nonrequired* 2004. It appears here by permission of the University of Nebraska Press. Copyright 2003 by the University of Nebraska Press. "The Boots" was originally published in *Story Quarterly* 42. It was also the winner of the 2005 Joseph Henry Jackson Award from the San Francisco Foundation and Intersection for the Arts. "Circus Night" was originally published as "Wire" in *Indiana Review* 24.2 (Fall 2002). "Groundskeeping" was originally published in *Glimmer Train* 40 (Fall 2001). "The Problem with Flight" was originally published in *Black Warrior Review* 28.2 (Spring/Summer 2002). "Coyotes" was originally published in *Indiana Review* 29.1 (Summer 2007).